"Forget it," Gray told her

How could she do this to him? He never lost his cool. *Till now in this damn jail cell.*

He started to pace. He was jealous. Incredible as it seemed, he'd decked Billy because he was jealous over another man paying attention to Sunny, a woman he would never have a relationship with, and who'd caused him more trouble in the past four days than any other woman had caused him in his whole damn life. And that was covering one hell of a lot of territory for Gray McBride.

He glanced at her from the corner of his eye, knowing he wanted to kiss her again no matter how much trouble she caused him. He puffed out a deep breath.

"It's going to be a long, long night," he said with a sigh.

D0017986

Hi, Everyone!

A Cowboy and a Kiss is truly a book of my heart. It's a lot of fun, a lot of sass and a whole lot of romance—just the sort of book I love to write.

When conservative lawyer Sophie gets thumped on the head and suddenly thinks she's showgirl Sunny from Reno, the fun begins. Except for Gray, who has to run for mayor and tries to keep Sunny—or is that Sophie?— in line without falling in love with her.

Add a loan shark, some washed-up cowboys who need jobs and a saloon that's supposed to be turned into a firehouse and this little Texas town will never be the same.

Kick back and come to Tranquility, Texas, where nothing's tranquil and Sophie and Gray beat the odds and fall hopelessly in love.

Enjoy!

Dianne Castell

P.S. I'd love hearing from you. Write me at DianneCastell@hotmail.com.

A COWBOY AND A KISS
Dianne Castell

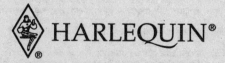

TORONTO • NEW YORK • LONDON
AMSTERDAM • PARIS • SYDNEY • HAMBURG
STOCKHOLM • ATHENS • TOKYO • MILAN • MADRID
PRAGUE • WARSAW • BUDAPEST • AUCKLAND

To Emily, who's practically perfect in every way.
And to Roberta Brown—best agent and wonderful friend.

ISBN 0-373-75051-X

A COWBOY AND A KISS

ABOUT THE AUTHOR

Dianne Castell is an empty-nester and lives in Milford, Ohio, with her retired husband and spoiled cat. She's given up cooking and cleaning and now spends that time yakking on the phone and online with authors Lori Foster and Leigh Riker. Her only regret is that she didn't do this years ago.

Books by Dianne Castell

HARLEQUIN AMERICAN ROMANCE

Don't miss any of our special offers. Write to us at the following address for information on our newest releases.

Harlequin Reader Service
U.S.: 3010 Walden Ave., P.O. Box 1325, Buffalo, NY 14269
Canadian: P.O. Box 609, Fort Erie, Ont. L2A 5X3

Chapter One

Sophie Addison drove into the Gas 'n' Go, dragged herself from the rental car, pushed damp curls from her forehead and kicked the front tire. "Worthless piece of donkey dung."

She swiped Texas sweat from her forehead and tugged at her pink spandex short-shorts and halter top, ungluing them from her soggy body. A tire smudge now marred her white sparkly flip-flops. Not exactly Reno business-attorney chic, but cooler than the suit she'd worn on the plane and the only thing in her size at the truck stop when her blasted AC died a hundred miles back. She jabbed the gas nozzle into the tank, clicked the auto-fuel and guzzled her sixth bottle of Evian water.

She'd get Sunny for this. For persuading Sophie to leave her administrative assistant the phone message from hell, saying she'd be out of town for two days and to reschedule *everything*. Mira just *loved* messages like that. Sophie made a mental note to send her flowers…with chocolates. Chocolates had gotten Sophie

out of more than one mess with Mira since joining
Burns, Lock, Trenton and Fowler, the best financial attorneys in Reno, five years ago.

Why couldn't Sunny be an attorney instead of an
impulsive, free-spirited, fun-loving Reno showgirl?
Sophie pictured her best friend since kindergarten as
an attorney in a black Anne Klein suit and bit back a
laugh. But no attorney with one ounce of gray matter
between her ears would borrow ten thousand dollars
from Cement Sam to bet on Showgirl Sunny in the fifth
at Santa Anita and really think the horse would win. So
Sunny wanted to buy into a casino of her own. That was
great, but not this way! *What was she thinking!*

Then Sophie spied a hunky cowboy at the next
pump and couldn't believe what *she* was thinking. Tall,
tanned, hat pulled low, great butt. Not that it mattered,
since she'd only be in Tranquility, Texas, long enough
to sell off the old saloon Sunny had inherited so the
town could expand their fire department. Then Sophie
had to get the money to Sam before he found Sunny
hiding out in Sophie's apartment in Reno with a
Reader's Digest and Oreos for company. Some plan!
Tom Clancy would not approve.

Sophie checked her watch. Sunny was already thir-
teen hours and forty-two minutes late with her payment, and the *cement* part of Sam's name didn't mean
he put in patios for a living, *unless* the person who re-
neged on his…or her…loan was *under* that patio.

Sophie swallowed, her mouth dryer than before.
What if Sam found Sunny before Sophie got the money

to him? That was why Sunny had chickened out of coming to Tranquility herself at the last minute. She'd decided to lay low, keep out of sight, tell the casino where she danced that she'd sprained her ankle. Then she'd gotten Sophie to run her little errand.

But what if Sophie couldn't close this sale for some reason? *And why couldn't she stop ogling the hunky cowboy?*

Sophie downed more water. Whatever possessed Sunny to borrow money from a loan shark to bet on a horse to get the money she wanted? It sure wasn't an approach Sophie would have taken. Other than blond hair and green eyes, the only things she and Sunny had in common were an Oreo and Coke addiction and departed aunts. Sophie's hadn't willed her a saloon, but after her parents had split to be Hollywood movie stars, Auntie had taken her in…along with every stray dog, cat, relative and kid who landed on their doorstep.

Someday Sophie intended to do that very thing as payback to Auntie for her kindness and caring. She intended to make her aunt proud.

The pump did a slow gurgle. She should ask the cowboy for directions to the saloon and courthouse. Her outfit lacked a certain respectability…understatement of the day…but this guy was definitely the best thing to come her way since Sunny had shown up on her doorstep last night in a panic.

What the heck. If Sunny got the Oreos, she got the cowboy. Boring, nose-to-the-grindstone attorneys were entitled to a little fun…even if only for five minutes.

GRAY MCBRIDE ANGLED his Stetson to block the blasting sun, smacked the old fuel pump twice to get it going, then set it to fill his pickup. He took his little black book from his back pocket, ripped out the *A* page and tossed it into a rusting steel drum. Goodbye, Sherry Abrams; farewell, Donna Ahern, Jenny Amirez and all the lovely *A* ladies. He sighed, then ripped out the *B* page. Great gals, good times, gone forever.

He tore the *C* page, then the *D* and bade adios to Barbara, Denise, Letta—*oh, how he'd miss Letta*—and the rest. He primed himself for a future of responsibility and running for mayor to prove once and for all to his pigheaded brother he could help run the ranch. Dillon needed to spend more time with his family. Today the twins were three; tomorrow they'd be in college and Dillon would wonder where the time had gone.

From now on, only mature, staid, settled women for Gray McBride. Accountants, lawyers, businesswomen who'd fit into his new lifestyle, embrace it with every fiber of their lackluster being. At least, that was his plan till he spied the sexy, spandex-wearing, gold-hair-flying babe at the other pump.

His heart did a little jig. *No!* He was twenty-nine; his jigging days were over. How could life be so cruel as to put such a beautiful, intriguing woman in his path now? Who was she? That Reno showgirl here to sell The Smokehouse? No one here dressed like that, and Cindy at the bank said they expected the owner in the next few days because she wanted to sell right away.

What was the rush, since she'd inherited the property some months ago? Guess she need the cash, though from what he could see…and he could see pretty darn much…she didn't need one damn thing.

So this is what Reno showgirls looked like. He had to get to Reno—*soon.* Then he remembered those days were over, too. Places like Houston and Dallas, and wearing suits and ties, loomed in his future. *Dang.*

"Hi," she said as she came his way. "I'm new here. Do you know where The Smokehouse saloon is? And the courthouse?"

"You're here to sell or partake?" He smiled. He could still smile at a pretty, sexy woman, couldn't he?

"I'm on the selling side. Thought I'd like to take a look at the place to make sure I'm getting the best price and—"

"Oh, holy hell." Gray shook his head and peered at the ground.

"There's something wrong with that? I'm not here to gouge anyone or make a killing or—"

"Gasoline." He pointed at a puddle forming. "Your car tank's overflowing. The pumps here are older than prairie dust. No automatic turnoff and—"

"Howdy, Gray," said an older man with a slight limp, coming up to the cowboy. He caught sight of the gal, his eyes bulged, jaw dropped and the cigarette dangling from the corner of his mouth somersaulted into the air as Gray yelled, *"No!"*

He grabbed for the cigarette, missed, and it landed

in the stream of gas, igniting like an angry dragon breathing fire at his truck…then the babe's car.

"*Yikes!*" She jumped back and shook her water bottle into the flames. He snagged her around the waist and the three of them dived behind the metal drums as an explosion sounded, the ground shook and he caught a last glimpse of Lucky Tanner's Gas 'n' Go igniting into one giant Texas barbecue pit.

AN HOUR LATER, Gray's head still pounded like a jackhammer on concrete. Lying in the clinic examining room, dressed in a hospital gown made for elves, with a flashlight glaring into his eyeball didn't make him feel one speck better. "Dang, Doc, you trying to blind me?"

"Just checking you out. But I can't say doing you bodily harm hasn't crossed my mind a time or two over the years."

He peered over his glasses, secured in the middle with a Flintstones Band-Aid. "That was *you* I caught with my Sue Ellen behind the woodpile, wasn't it, looking all goo-goo eyed?"

Gray sighed; the pounding increased. "And like I've told you for the past *fifteen years*, we were looking for Venus. It was a science project and Sue Ellen's lab partner weaseled out on her. She's married, Doc, and you're sixty and have two grandkids. Give it up."

Doc clicked off his flashlight. His toupee slid a bit off center, his eyes turned steely and his lips thinned to a straight line. "And if I had an ounce of proof you *found* Venus with my Sue Ellen, you'd be deader then a carp in a cup of spit."

"So you've said, over and over…" *What was the use?* Doc would never understand that Gray could be with a gal and not be scheming how to get her in bed. Gray took stock of the cuts and scrapes Doc had treated with something that stung like a barrelful of hornets— retaliation for the Venus incident, no doubt—and cleared his throat. "Norm and the lady okay?"

"Norm's all right. Left a few minutes ago. And you're fine as frog's hair. The gal's sleeping. Her car got vaporized to pixie dust, and if you hadn't snagged her when you did and those steel drums not been in place to protect you from the blast, you all would have gone up in smoke. One jim-dandy of a fire, yessiree."

"The gal's all right, then?"

"Groggy when the EMS folks brought her in, talk- ing about The Smokehouse and getting smudges on her new shoes, then she fell asleep. Probably knocked her head when you all dived for your lives. A slight concus- sion, some scrapes and bruises, but that's all. Too bad about her car."

Car? Gray forgot about the stinging hornets and skimpy gown. "What about *my* new surround-sound, four-wheel-drive with custom-metallic red-paint pick- up? Any word on *that*?"

Doc stepped into the hall and returned with a crunched steering wheel. "Little present from the boys at the fire department. Since you're trying to get them a better firehouse and all."

Gray felt his eyebrows shoot to his hairline. "That's *it*?"

Doc's eyebrows fused. "Least I'm not holding up one of your body parts, cowboy. And you still got your hat, so quit your bellyaching." He snatched the battered black Stetson from the chair and blew off the dust, sending a small cloud into the room. He handed the hat to Gray.

Gray stuck his finger through one of the holes. "It was my daddy's."

"Well, now it's ventilated. Fared better than Lucky's Gas 'n' Go. Flatter than a bullfrog on the four-lane."

Gray puffed out a breath of air and ran his hand through his slightly fried hair. "Maybe now everyone will understand *why* I'm campaigning to expand our fire department. Pumper trucks and some outdated hoses aren't enough."

He set the Stetson to the back of his head. The brim sagged over his left eye.

"Election's in a little over two weeks. I suppose you got time to show people you're not just a hell-raising cowboy and you'd be good at running Tranquility. You *could* get elected mayor. Age of miracles isn't dead." Doc opened a manila folder. "Says here you're due for a tetanus shot."

"Your confidence in my ability is overwhelming. Hell, I'm closing my favorite saloon so the firehouse behind can expand into it. That'll make Tranquility real damn tranquil, probably more than it's been since Longhorn Jones founded the place a hundred years ago. And it'll give us a better firehouse. That's all got to count for something."

He rubbed his sore shoulder. "I'm in no mood for a shot. I'll stop by tomorrow "

"Now's as good a time as any for getting your records current." Doc picked a syringe with a needle that seemed at least four inches long. This day was not getting any better, and he bit back a yelp as Doc jabbed him. Just what he needed—a little more pain in his life. Next time he inoculated a calf he'd show some sympathy.

"Can I go see the lady while I'm waiting for one of the hands from the ranch to bring me some clothes? Feel kind of responsible."

"I'll be along in a minute to check on her. I best be telling Ms. Rose I'm running late here, or she'll feed my dinner to the dogs before she heads out to one of her volunteer meetings. Why I hired her as my housekeeper is a mystery to me."

"Because she bakes the best peach pie in Texas and at sixty still turns a head or two when she walks down the street."

Doc reddened, muttered something about not caring about Ms. Rose turning heads and started for his office. Gray chuckled, holding his sore ribs. He snatched another gown, slid it on robe style and walked down the hall to room 103.

He pushed open the door and studied the small, vulnerable woman under the white sheet. But she really wasn't all that small. He'd only topped her by a few inches. That made her about five-nine or so. Not skinny, more medium. She had a scrape on her forehead and nose. Other than that she looked…fine. Fine indeed.

Gold curls, slightly singed at the ends, trailed across the pillow. He was a sucker for long blond hair. Always had been. He remembered green eyes big as softballs when the three of them had made a flying leap over the steel drums. He thought of pink shorts and top tantalizing the hell out of him.

A Reno showgirl was not in any way an asset to his campaign *or* to the family image he needed to make it all work, and that was a damn shame. He sighed, touched her cheek and bade the golden-haired beauty goodbye.

SHE WAS DREAMING…a really great dream. Someone was touching her cheek, making her feel warm all over. She eased her eyes open…gazing into big brown eyes gazing into her.

A man. A real one, not a dream at all, looming over her. And she was lying flat on her back in bed. A hospital bed. What the heck was she doing here? *What was he doing here?*

She gasped, and he pulled back his hand. Thank heavens! Though her brain was the only part doing the thanking. Then he smiled and her brain knew it had made a mistake.

"Feeling better?"

"Why…why am I in a hospital bed? Why do I feel

I've been blindsided by a Mack truck? Are you a doctor? Why are you wearing a cowboy hat…with a hole?"

His eyebrows knit into a confused frown. He had
great eyes, the kind with a little twinkle. *I-love-life*
kind of eyes. Who was this handsome man? Her head
hurt like mad. Everything throbbed. Nothing made
sense. Though when she looked at him she didn't care
quite so much.

"Doc Lamont will be here in a minute. We—you
and I—met at the Gas 'n' Go. I'm the guy you shared
that explosion with."

"Explosion?" Her eyes widened, then she scrunched
them back to normal because they hurt.

"Gasoline? Overflowed? You tried to put the fire out
with your Evian and—"

She pulled in a deep breath. "Slow down. I…I don't
have a clue what you're talking about."

His grin slipped a notch. "You *do* remember asking
me for directions to The Smokehouse and courthouse,
don't you?"

"Guess I didn't find either one, huh?"

He took her hand. Warm, reassuring, strong. "This
is Tranquility, Texas." He sat on the edge of her bed.
"Your brain's scrambled, that's all."

She looked around the unfamiliar room and an un-
easy feeling crept up her spine. The man pushed his dilapidated hat back on his head. "Same thing happened
to me enough times when I rode rodeo and got tossed
by a bull. Once I landed so hard I was two inches
shorter than when I started and I couldn't remember my

own name." He chuckled, then said, "I'm Gray McBride. And you are...?"

Uneasiness accelerated to panic.

He gripped her hand tighter. "Don't go getting yourself in a lather over forgetting a few details."

She exhaled a deep breath to stay calm, not wanting to be bitchy or rude. *"Not knowing who I am is not a little detail."*

"You really can't remember?"

"Oh, gee, I feel so much better now." *So much for not being bitchy or rude.*

The door opened and an older man with a bad toupee and a white lab coat scurried in. Doc Lamont?

"Well, now," he said. "You're awake and talking. Mighty glad to see that. Mighty glad indeed."

"Don't get too overjoyed. I...I can't remember anything. My name, where I'm from...zip. Now what? You give me a shot or something and I'm all better?"

The cowboy tipped back his hat. "Wouldn't recommend the shot."

Doc said to Gray, "You can go, cowboy. Stop back in tomorrow so I can check you over again."

"I'm the last person she talked to and she's kind of disoriented. Maybe I should stay."

"If you're feeling up to it." He took off his watch and handed it to her. "What time it is?"

"Six twenty-five." She glanced out the window at the setting sun. "That's p.m. Why can I remember that and not who I am? *What's wrong with me? What am I going to do?"*

Doc shone his penlight into one eye, then the other. "This is just a little temporary forgetfulness brought on by a conk on the head. Nothing serious, or you'd have other symptoms. Your brain's been bruised. It needs time to heal. And it will."

"Where's my stuff? Purse, ID? Every woman has a purse and ID. That will jog some memory loose."

Doc stroked his chin. "Didn't make it."

The cowboy said, "But I know who you are. We talked before the explosion. You're a showgirl from Reno. You're Sunny Kelly."

Her jaw dropped a fraction. "Showgirl? What would a Reno showgirl be doing here in Texas?"

"You inherited a saloon, The Smokehouse, from your aunt Bessy. No one in town even knew she had a niece till a couple of months ago, when the attorney over at the bank read the will. Since I'm running for mayor of Tranquility, I proposed contacting you to see if you were interested in selling so we could expand our firehouse, which is located right behind it. We didn't hear anything for several weeks, then two days ago you phoned and said you wanted to sell and would fly in."

"I did?"

"When we were at the gas pump you told me that's why you were here."

She massaged her temples and closed her eyes. "Sunny? Smokehouse? Showgirl? A kind aunt? Auntie?" She shook her head. "Sort of sounds familiar, especially the aunt part. But look at me." She spread her arms wide. "A Reno showgirl?"

The cowboy grinned. "You were wearing hot-pink spandex."

Again she willed herself to stay calm. This was not the time for hysterics, no matter who she was or what she wore. "I've got to tell you, I can't even think of a single dance step." She nibbled her bottom lip. "Pink spandex, huh?"

"And glittery flip-flops."

She rolled her eyes. "Not only a showgirl but one with questionable taste."

Doc patted her shoulder. "When you're good and ready you'll remember. Until then, things are going to be kind of mixed up and confusing because your memory will come back in snatches. Just trust your instincts and you'll be okay. We'll all watch out for you."

"Just don't let me buy any more spandex."

"But you *are* Sunny Kelly," insisted the cowboy. *What was his name? Gray?* He continued, "And as soon as you're up to it, you can finalize the sale of The Smokehouse and be on a plane back to Reno and I can get on with my campaign promise to enlarge the firehouse."

"That's for later," Doc said. "Right now you need rest. Gray and I are leaving, but there's a nurse on duty and she'll be checking on you from time to time." He nodded, his eyes reassuring. "Try not to worry. Everything's going to be fine as frog's hair."

She watched the door close behind the doctor and the cowboy and gazed out the window at the sunset. At least she knew it was a sunset. And that she had an aunt.

Dear Auntie. Just the name made her feel warm with love and sadness that she was gone.

How could this happen? And how could that cowboy unsettle her so? Okay, that was an easy question to answer. Those brown eyes would unsettle Alan Greenspan.

Yikes! What kind of showgirl couldn't remember one dance step but kept the head of the Federal Reserve on the tip of her tongue? Why did she even know about the Federal Reserve? Because she had one big mixedup case of amnesia, that was why, and maybe she'd read about Al somewhere.

So what should she do until her memory came back? Keep busy, really busy. Why in the world did she have to get amnesia in the first place? Then again, anyone who wore spandex deserved amnesia.

THE NEXT AFTERNOON, Gray stood on the sidewalk under the big oak in front of The Smokehouse. Time to get on with his plans for the saloon. Not only because he wanted it sold to allow for expansion of the firehouse behind it, but because he wanted Sunny Kelly *gone*.

For the past two days, he'd thought about her. Nice shape, green eyes, long, wonderful silky hair…except for the fried ends. How was he supposed to consider dating sensible, sedate women to prove he was a changed man to the town and his brother with tempting showgirl Sunny around?

There was a light in the saloon. Doc said she'd

checked herself out of the clinic and was now staying here, hoping something might jog her memory. He felt bad about that. If he'd done something differently, maybe she wouldn't have hit her head. Except there'd been no time. The three of them were damn lucky not to be crispy critters.

Gray stepped onto the boot-worn porch, felt the familiar sag of rotting boards underfoot and went inside. "Anybody home?"

The odor of stale beer and old cigarette smoke washed over him, reminding him of some really great times, like when he'd turned twenty-one and big brother Dillon had brought him to The Smokehouse for his first beer. Make that first *legal* beer. He owed Dillon for being a great big brother and step-in dad after their father had died. Mom had been devastated and twenty-one-year-old Dillon had taken on running the ranch and fifteen-year-old Gray…and saving both. Now Gray intended to pay Dillon back, *if* he could just convince Dillon he was up to it. Being mayor was a last-ditch effort.

"Mr. McBride?" Sunny Kelly sat at the bar. "What can I do for you?"

"You…you cut your hair. It was so…" *Beautiful, golden, silky.* "Long."

She shrugged. "Frizzed ends. Like I'd been used for a lightning rod."

He'd strangle the barber. How could anyone cut her hair? And she wore baggy jeans and a T-shirt. Bessy's, no doubt. What he wouldn't give for another glimpse of her in spandex. *Or not. Get a grip, McBride. No sexy women, remember?* They were off his radar forever.

His job right now was to soften up Sunny Kelly—not ogle her. Get the saloon sold for the cheapest price, leaving more money to renovate the firehouse. He glanced around and sighed. "Wow. This place is sure a shambles. It'd take a fortune to fix it up."

"I heard that," came a female voice from the other end of the bar.

In the dim light—and distracted by Sunny—he hadn't seen the other woman. *"Elizabeth?"*

Ah, hell. His great plan for a cheap sale went right up in flames. Sister-in-law Elizabeth wasn't the softening-up type, except when it came to her boys. How she kept up with them Gray couldn't imagine. Maybe that was why today she had her hair pulled back into a clip, her suit was rumpled with a stain shaped like a little hand on the front of her blouse and she had on two different earrings and a purple dinosaur peeking out of her pocket. Not the pristine attorney of five years ago, but a great mother.

He leaned against the bar. "What are you doing here?"

Sunny nodded at the papers in front of her. "Elizabeth's father is president of the bank that holds the mortgage on the saloon. When I talked to him this morning, he said he'd send an attorney over to explain what was what before I signed the sale papers."

Gray asked Elizabeth. "Where are the twins? I don't think I've seen you without them since they were born. What's going on?"

Sunny's eyes widened. "You have twins?"

Elizabeth grinned. "Three-year-old boys. Ben and Joey." Her voice turned dreamy. "Sweetest, most darling—"

"Trouble times two," Gray added with a chuckle. "She's my sister-in-law."

Elizabeth winked at Sunny. "The twins favor their uncle Gray."

Gray asked, "Did Dillon take the day off to watch the kids?"

"Your brother take a day off? When cows fly. He's still in Amarillo. I taped his picture to a kitchen chair so the kids can eat dinner with their father. Your mom and my dad and three of the ranch hands are baby-sitting. They threw me out of the house—my own house—to come down here. Said I needed to get my mind on something besides kids. That I needed to think about something else besides the ABC song and Builder Bob, and maybe work would help."

She sighed. "All this because I just happened to cut up my father's meat when he came for dinner last week and put his milk in a sippy cup."

Elizabeth reached around in her big purse and pulled out a package of wipes, two boxes of raisins and three toy cars. She held up a cell phone, grinning in triumph. "Think I'll see how everyone's doing."

Sunny shrugged. "It's five adults for two kids."

Elizabeth gritted her teeth and sucked in a breath. "I know, but that's all the adults they could come up with on short notice."

As Elizabeth spoke on the phone, Gray nodded at the papers. "Everything in order?"

"Wish I remembered Bessy better." Sunny rubbed her hands over her face. "I feel she was a warm, caring person."

"How about cantankerous and ornery? That's a little closer to true."

Sunny pulled herself up tall and her lips formed a straight line. "I don't think so. Maybe she just kept her goodness and kindness a secret. Some people do that, you know."

"Best-kept secret in town. But, hey." He held up his hands in surrender. No need to poke the bear…he wanted the saloon cheap. "If you remember Bessy as kind and caring, that's fine with me." He nudged the bill of sale lying on the bar. "Seems a fair price."

Sunny studied it and played with a strand of her hair as if trying to get used to it being short. He stuffed his hands in his pockets to keep from touching. He was suddenly a sucker for *short* blond hair.

"Doesn't seem right to sell Bessy's pride and joy and take the money and run back to Reno. Just doesn't seem right."

Oh, no. Not a guilt trip. Guilt trips made people do dumb things they wouldn't ordinarily do…like not sell saloons when they should.

Gray waved his hand over the interior. "The Smokehouse wasn't an element of pride for Bessy. More like basic income to go gamble in Vegas. And I don't remember her ever being…*joyous*."

Sunny closed her eyes and shook her head. "It doesn't matter. I can't run this place alone, and I don't know the town or the people. I don't even know me. What else *can* I do but sell?"

Gray gave a mental sigh of relief as Elizabeth dropped her phone back in her purse and said, "I have to get back to the ranch. The kids locked two of the ranch hands in the attic, then flushed the key down the toilet and hid my father's glasses." She said to Sunny, "You can meet with the town council at the bank this afternoon and hammer out the details. I'll set things up."

She scrounged a rumpled business card from her purse, wiped off a smear, smoothed it out and handed it to Sunny. Then she left.

This was great, Gray thought. Things were moving along just the way he'd hoped. He could leave now, his work done. After Sunny signed the papers this afternoon, the firehouse was as good as expanded...*if* he got elected. He started for the door, pictured short blond hair and green eyes and slowly turned back to Sunny.

"You wanted something else, Mr. McBride?"

Yeah. He wanted to touch her again. How dumb was that? "You made a good choice. And the name's Gray."

Actually, his name was *Stupid* because he could feel himself being attracted to Sunny Kelly. Her luscious hair, great eyes, womanly curves, and the way she protected an aunt she didn't even remember. It didn't matter whether Bessy was Mother Teresa or Attila the Hun; it was how Sunny stood up for her that intrigued Gray. He didn't need to be intrigued by a woman so completely wrong for him. What he needed was Sunny Kelly gone from Tranquility. "After you sign the papers this afternoon I can give you a lift to the airport. I have a truck right outside."

"What am I going to do in Reno once I get there? I still can't remember one single dance step. Here, watch."

She twirled, crashed into the stool, ricocheted off that and collided into Gray. He caught her to keep them both from falling over.

"See what I mean?"

She felt wonderful in his arms, the tantalizing warmth of her breath and the heat from her body flowing into his. She was addictive.

She smiled, his heartbeat doubled and he did a mental head slap. *Get a grip!* He steadied her and took a step back. "Tell you what. I'll spring for the ticket to Reno myself. You won't have to cash the check for the sale of the saloon till you get home."

"But I can't dance."

"Dance?"

She huffed. "Sunny Kelly? Once-upon-a-time Reno dancer? Me? What the heck am I going to do in Reno if I can't be a showgirl? And where *is* home?"

"You can find it in the phone book." He tried to focus on something besides the incredibly lovely woman he'd held in his arms. "I just bet once you're in Reno, you'll remember everything. Familiar surroundings and people will jar your memory."

He couldn't take his eyes off her. She mesmerized him. The way she moved with a little sway in her hips; the way she tilted her head when she was thinking about her past. Her energy, which filled every nook and cranny of the dark dingy bar and seemed to make it come alive. She was a fresh breeze blowing through Tranquility. Ah, hell! *No fresh breezes.*

She crinkled her nose—her very cute nose. "What if the town built a firehouse somewhere else?"

He worked to concentrate on her words and not her. "Building a completely new firehouse is too expensive. Renovations to this place are less since the firehouse is right behind the saloon and we can just connect the two buildings. Use this place for storage and buy a new rig. We've money enough for that. I intend to close The Smokehouse as part of my campaign promise to make the town safer, more family oriented. The Smokehouse is a rowdy cowboy saloon."

"And I just bet you know this from firsthand experience, right?"

"See that chair?" He pointed to the corner. "Has my name on the back. Won it from Bessy in a poker game. But that's all part of my past. My brother, Dillon, needs my help running our ranch so he can be a real father and not just a picture taped to a chair."

Gray raked back his hair. "I've worked on proving to him I'm capable by going to cattle meetings with him, sitting in on discussions about the oil rigs, suggesting new herds and property we should buy, but he dismisses whatever I say. He thinks I'm too young and inexperienced to know what I'm talking about. I'm always *little brother,* even at twenty-nine. The fact that he took over everything at twenty-one doesn't faze him. I figure if he realizes I can run the whole damn town for the next two years he'll come to the conclusion I can help run the ranch. I don't know what else to do to convince him."

Sunny shrugged. "Just tell him you're taking over some of the responsibility. It's a family ranch—you're part of the family. You wouldn't have to run for mayor. Somehow you don't look like the political type."

"It's not that simple. When Dad died, Dillon left grad school, moved home and made it the success it is now. He took on a lot of responsibility, including me. I want Dillon to give me responsibility because he believes I can do the job. I owe him for shouldering a load…and a lot more."

She was quiet for a moment…too quiet. Then she said, "A noble quest for you, Mr. McBride, but not for me." She ran her hand over a paint-chipped tabletop and gazed out the dirty window.

Uh-oh. This was not a woman packing things in and heading for the airport. This was a woman *bonding.* "Bet you're noble as hell back in Reno."

She faced him. "Bessy left me the bar, entrusted it to me. You don't want to let Dillon down. I don't want to let Auntie down by just selling something she gave me. I don't think of her as being a sellout sort of person."

Sunny held out her hands, palms up. "Besides, I don't remember how to dance, so what in the world would I ever do in Reno?"

Drive every man there nuts, instead of me. "Look at this place. It's a total dump. You're a showgirl. Sexy as hell. Wear skimpy clothes, feathers, heels, sequins. You belong on the stage in Reno." Dang, he was turning himself on just talking about her. He had to get rid of Sunny Kelly. "If you don't want to sell, there are ways to force the issue. The town needs the firehouse. They could get...pushy."

She put her hands to her hips, and her lips pulled into a pucker. Did it have to be a pucker?

"Or are *you* the one getting pushy?"

"There's eminent domain. Where the individual has to sell for the good of all the people. The firehouse is for the good of all."

She tossed her head and jutted her chin. "I know all about eminent domain."

"You do? You really remember that?"

She paused and stared off into space. A little smile tipped her lips and she said. "Yeah, I do. Least, I remember *something*." She focused on Gray. "Guess I'm a smarter showgirl than you bargained for."

"This place should be condemned. If that happens, you'll have no business to run and you won't get nearly as much money as you would if you sold to the town right now. What will you do if that happens?"

"Not vote for you for mayor?"

"Dammit, Sunny Kelly. You're a blasted showgirl. Go back to Reno. *You can't run a saloon.*"

"Gray McBride, bite me!"

Chapter Two

Blast the woman. Gray glared at Sunny across the room. Hard to be pissed off at such a beautiful gal, but he was working on it. How could she tick him off and tantalize him both at the same time?

She pushed her hair back from her face as she peered at him. "The Smokehouse needs a little updating, that's all. I could paint the tables and chairs. Cream and hunter green would be nice."

"Yeah, cowboys just love that cream-and-hunter-green stuff. What it needs is new wiring, plumbing and a roof, and that costs a lot of money. Bessy was no businesswoman. You can't afford it."

"I'll get rid of the strange-looking couch thing over there—" she nodded across the room "—surrounded by those big ugly orange mats. What kind of decor is that? I can find something more attractive."

Hell, she wasn't listening to him at all. She'd shifted from bonding mode to nesting. "That decor is *cowboy*. And it's not a couch—it's a mechanical bull. Meet Widow Maker. The mats are so cowboys don't break their dang-fool necks when they get tossed off the thing."

Her eyes sparked. "*Ha.* You think I'm a total ditz because I'm a showgirl from Reno. Where's the head and tail? What kind of bull, mechanical or otherwise, doesn't have a head or tail?"

He rolled his eyes so far back he saw his tonsils. He sauntered over to the bar and flipped a switch to start the action, making her gasp and stumble back. *"Yikes."*

He arched an eyebrow and leaned against the bar. "And *you're* going to run a cowboy bar?"

She jutted her chin. "Dear sweet Auntie thought I was up to the task or she wouldn't have left me the place."

"You're her only living relative. This is not bequeathing the family jewels. And, like I said, *Auntie* was not sweet. Try crotchety…and that was on a good day."

Sunny huffed, "Then you didn't know my aunt very well at all."

"And you did?"

"Maybe…when I was little, and then our families lost touch. Or something like that. It makes sense." She ran her hand through her short hair. "But how the heck should I know. *I have amnesia.*"

She was a complete pain and he was drawn to her like a cat to cream. What the hell was he going to do if she stayed and he felt this way every time he looked at her?

"I admit I'd have to learn a few things."

Why couldn't Don Rickles have been the one to pull into town and get amnesia? Gray would never be attracted to Don Rickles. "What about the fire department? Is this saloon more important than the town having a decent fire department?"

She pursed her lips and he wanted nothing more than to see if they were soft, moist and a prefect match for his. She said, "No, it's not," and let out a deep breath. "You're right. A fire department is more important than a saloon. People are more important."

"The town council should have the papers drawn up by this afternoon, like Elizabeth said. You can sign them, get your money and be out of here. I'm glad you see things my way."

HA! SHE DIDN'T SEE things his way. She just couldn't think of a good argument against the firehouse at the moment. Sentimental feelings couldn't win out over people's welfare even with someone who had amnesia.

Sunny watched Gray cross the saloon floor, open the wooden door and close it behind him. She picked up a dented tin ashtray off the bar and threw it against the door. *"Damnation."*

"That's one way to say goodbye," came a voice from behind.

She spun around, facing a man and woman she didn't know. Though, considering her present state of mind, that covered a lot of territory. Both were young— early twenties at best—holding hands, baby on the way.

"I'm Jerome Smith, Smitty, barkeep around here for two years now until Bessy croak—I mean passed. And this is Jean. Barmaid…when she's up to it. He draped his arm around her and held her close.

Smitty scuffed the toe of his worn boot against the floor. "We—Jean and me—ran the saloon for Bessy. She let us stay in the basement and we just sort of hung on after the place closed. Apartments are real expensive. We kind of paid our way by keeping poachers from sneaking in and helping themselves to whiskey and the like. The sheriff's been watching the place, too."

Smitty pointed to a closed door off to the side. "Jean and I fixed our place up nice. Hope you don't mind. I'm guessing you're Bessy's niece. Here to take a look around before you sell?"

"Thanks for taking care of The Smokehouse. Auntie would have wanted you to stay, and I'm glad you did. Though she's starting to sound a bit more feisty than I remember…*or don't remember*."

Jean chuckled, her blue eyes sparkling. "No one else would work for Bessy but us. We really needed the jobs." She unconsciously ran a protective hand over her rounded middle.

Sunny hitched herself onto a stool, propped her elbow on the bar and rested her chin in her palm. This young couple needed The Smokehouse to stay open. If it closed they'd not only lose their jobs but their home. Yet how could she keep it going? "Let's line up our ducks. The firehouse needs the saloon for expansion, the books are on life support, the only real value is the land, but it could qualify for a second mortgage and give us a narrow cash flow for repairs and minimum wages. Even though you both know the town, and that's a big help, and I know how to construct a circular-flow diagram, offset restrictive practices determined by the town council and develop a market-equilibrium plan, I'm not sure that would be enough to make a go of this place."

Her eyes bulged and her chin slid out of her palm. Smitty said, "Huh?" and Jean followed with, "*Heavenly days*. Do you have any idea what all that gibberish you just rattled off means?"

Sunny laughed. A real laugh that seemed to come from her toes and felt good all over. "Yeah, I really do. I must have read it somewhere. *Reader's Digest*." She laughed again. "Yeah, that was it. I read *Reader's Digest*."

She remembered something! Something concrete. She sucked in a quick breath. *Yikes.* Why did that word, *concrete*, make her blood run cold? What was that all about? Another question to add to the long, long list. When Doc said she'd remember in snatches he wasn't kidding.

Smitty folded his arms. "Well, what else did you read?"

This all felt right, like something she should do, really wanted to do. Helping the young couple the way Auntie would have. "If we could turn this place around, I'd institute a profit-sharing plan, give you both a share of The Smokehouse. Auntie would have wanted that.

The big question is, how do we do it? How do we make this place pay for itself? Got any ideas?"

Smitty stared at her wide-eyed, swallowed and ran his hand over his face. "You're asking us? I got to be truthful with you. Most people around here think we're not good for much except serving up long necks. I'm just a washed-up cowboy." He patted his arm that didn't hang at a natural angle.

"You're what, twenty-two? You haven't had time to wash up."

"Twenty-three, and broncs don't ask how old you are when they trample your arm."

Sunny slid from the stool and paced. No way could she kick out this young family. Not only would Auntie hunt her down and haunt like some banshee ghost for the rest of her natural days, Sunny Kelly wasn't that kind of person in her own right. Amnesia or not, a person knew who she was deep inside.

A plan could help. Something to generate income. The pictures on the wall might suggest something. She took down a small one, blew off the dust, sending motes into the air. "Smitty? This *is* you."

He rolled his strong shoulders and nodded at the other pictures. "These are all the guys and gals in Tranquility who've done the rodeo circuit."

Jean said, "Smitty was a terrific bronc rider." She put her hand in his. "And now he's even better, least to me." She patted her rounded abdomen. "He took me and the baby in." She bit her bottom lip till it blanched white. "The baby's not his."

A cowboy, a hero and a real man, all at twenty-three.

Smitty reddened and shifted from one foot to the other, then nodded at a picture in the middle of the grouping. "Uh, there's Gray." Relief in his voice as he diverted attention from himself. "Mighty fine bull rider in his day. Went all the way to the finals in Pocatello, Idaho."

Jean giggled. "And every female north of the Rio Grande went right along with him. The gals sure like Gray. Treats every woman like a lady."

Sunny studied the picture. "Yeah, well, big brown eyes, broad shoulders and a nice butt don't hurt, either." She blushed. "Sorry, that just kind of slipped out. Probably from the amnesia." *How lame!*

"You know, with all this local talent and interest…maybe…maybe we could sponsor a rodeo. That would give The Smokehouse a new town-friendly image. And it would attract more customers, a diverse clientele."

Rodeo? Now, where did that come from? She took in Gray's cocky smile and macho cowboy stance. *Dumb question.*

Smitty shook his head. "Best time for a rodeo is the Fourth of July and that's less than two weeks away. Putting on a rodeo is a ton of hard work, even if we just do it for Tranquility."

"Hard work doesn't mean it's impossible. I am a showgirl. I have to remember something about entertainment, right? The Smokehouse can afford the advertising if we keep it simple. We'll have local groups do refreshments and get some ranch to donate cattle, since a rodeo's good for the whole town." She smacked her palm to her forehead. *"That's it.* The proceeds of the rodeo can build a new firehouse…somewhere else besides our saloon. Which ranch around here is the most philanthropic?"

Smitty laughed. "You just threw an ashtray at it."

Sunny closed her eyes. "My luck is not changing. Maybe if I bury garlic upside down under a full moon things will turn around."

This time Jean laughed. "It's going to take more than buried garlic to get Gray McBride to give up his plans for a firehouse and getting elected mayor."

And the next morning as Sunny drove out to Gray's ranch, the Lazy K, she knew Jean was right. It was nice of Smitty to lend her his Nova and the sheriff to give her a temporary driver's license after establishing that Sunny Kelly did indeed have a driver's license—and two speeding tickets in the past year.

But that was the least of her problems. Right now she had to get Gray to think rodeo and not saloon. She took the turn that led between the two white gates with Lazy K printed neatly across the top rungs and headed for the rambling stone-and-clapboard house up ahead. The ranch was perfect. Not postcard perfect but working-ranch perfect, with people here and there doing ranchy things under a big blue Texas sky dotted with puffs of white clouds.

She pulled up next to the house with yellow roses trailing up one corner and baskets of pink geraniums hanging on the wraparound porch and swinging in the morning breeze. She killed the engine and got out as a big dog—or small horse—bounded her way, tail wagging like a windshield wiper stuck on superspeed. She stepped back, not because he scared her with his attitude so much as his size. "Stay. Sit. *Holy cow, don't jump!*"

To her amazement, he didn't. He stopped and sniffed her shoes, her knees and parts he shouldn't be sniffing at all. Dogs have no shame. He was black with white around one eye, one paw and at the tip of his tail. He flopped over on his back. "Good boy." She hunkered down. "Like to have your belly scratched?"

"Sometimes," came Gray's voice behind her. She turned and gazed up at him. "Decided to sell after all?"

With Gray McBride around, she couldn't decide on anything. He was too handsome, too distracting, too delicious to be around and keep her wits about her.

The dog whined for more attention as she stood. Then he jumped up and put his front paws on her shoulders, making them nose to nose. And one of theirs was wet.

Gray pulled off his hat and swiped his forehead. "So what are *you* doing here? Are the papers ready to be signed?"

"Not exactly. And I think I'm dancing with your dog, who has really bad breath."

"He's not mine. He's a stray. We call him Six because he's the sixth stray someone's dropped off this year—for us to find homes for them."

"Why do people do such things? Ditch their responsibilities. It's…terrible. Poor baby." For some reason she felt a connection to Six. She scratched him behind the ears and studied Gray out of the corner of her eye. A dusty, hardworking, strong, capable cowboy standing confidently on his own land, and caring for stray dogs made him the sexiest man alive. Though the hat could use a little work.

Six dropped down, then sat beside her. "I'm having a wake for Bessy tonight. Thought you might want to come since you have your own chair and all."

His eyes widened. "Is this one last fling before you sell the place off?"

"I have an idea for the town, something to draw attention to The Smokehouse and bring revenue to Tranquility. A rodeo. For the Fourth of July. Maybe you'd like to donate some of your cattle." She gave him a coy smile. "It could help your campaign since everyone around here loves rodeos."

"What happened to selling?"

She tried to look innocent. Except where Gray McBride was concerned, nothing that came to mind was innocent. He put his hands on his hips…his narrow hips accented by perfect-fitting jeans.

"I don't believe this. You really have a sense of humor, Sunny Kelly, I'll give you that. It's one thing you haven't lost. You want me to help you with a rodeo that will, somehow, benefit The Smokehouse, keep it open and sabotage my idea to enlarge the firehouse?"

He leaned against the Nova and laughed. He had a

great laugh, and she would have appreciated it a lot more if the laugh hadn't been directed at her.

She gave Gray an intimidating look, though it was tough to look intimidating while petting a big dog sitting on your foot. "If the rodeo is successful the town can build a whole new firehouse somewhere else. A rodeo would be good for Tranquility. Give it prestige. And think of the votes you'll get if your name's connected—"

Two little boys darted out the front door of the big house, running full tilt toward Gray across the grass, naked as the day they were born and yelling, "Uncle Gray, Uncle Gray, no bath, no bath."

A man in a dress shirt open at the throat and rolled at the sleeves, dress pants and intense but very tired brown eyes chased after them and swooped up one wiggly toddler, then the other. This was obviously *not* the first time he'd performed this feat.

"Hey, Dillon," Gray called as the man approached, the naked boys giggling and squirming. "If you're busy with the kids, I can take that meeting in Fort Worth tomorrow morning."

"I'm heading out tonight. Got it covered, little brother. Thanks." He nodded at Sunny, then headed back to the house with his charges.

Sunny stared at the house as the door closed behind the three males. Something deep inside her stirred. A home. She was homesick and couldn't even remember where home was. Did she have a family? A husband? Probably not. No wedding ring. And she wouldn't be so attracted to Gray.

"That was Dillon and the two reasons I need to help out around here." Gray shook his head. "There's no way I'm helping you with the rodeo that will keep the saloon open. The idea of a hastily-thrown-together rodeo generating enough money to build a new firehouse is chancy at best."

She let out a long sigh. "I do see your point. In fact, I even respect it."

He grinned, making her feel a bit lightheaded. "This means you're going to sell, right?"

"It means Ralph Nester, your worthy opponent for mayor, whose posters are all over town, is my next stop. I got the directions from the sheriff. The rodeo could be a real boost for him and his campaign. The firehouse is your idea, not his." She smiled sweetly. "See you tonight, Gray McBride."

She climbed back into the Nova, fired it up and rumbled back down the driveway. She glanced in the rearview mirror to get one last look at Gray. Instead, she saw the big black-and-white dog galloping toward the car, his tongue hanging happily from his mouth.

She slammed on the brakes and opened the passenger side of the Nova. She couldn't turn her back on him. In an instant the dog with bad breath and a dopey smile parked in the seat beside her, taking up more than his share of the front. So this is how Gray found homes for the strays…at least, this stray. "Get off the gearshift or we're not going anywhere. Why am I letting you in this car? Why am I buckling you into the seat? *Why am I talking to a dog like I expect him to answer?*"

His wagging tail thumped against the seat and he licked her face.

"*Yuck. Gross.* No more." He licked again. "Why couldn't you be a Chihuahua?"

THAT NIGHT GRAY parked the truck across the street from The Smokehouse and hopped out. Drizzle mixed with the warm night breeze. Streetlights cast round circles on the wet pavement. Since Sunny Kelly had blown—literally—into his life nothing was the same.

Why couldn't he be the one with amnesia? Life would be so much simpler if he could just forget about running for mayor, forget rodeos and forget the knockout showgirl who was dead set on saving a run-down saloon for dear Auntie. Where the heck did she get *that* idea?

A Willie Nelson song spilled from the open saloon doorway, and Gray stepped onto the porch, then went inside. He gave a nod of greeting to young Smitty, who sang along. Cowboys milled about inside, pool balls clacked, glasses and bottles clanked. Laughter mixed with the rise and fall of voices. Gray peered through the cigarette smoke. Bessy's wake? *Ha.* More like everyone wanted to get a glimpse of the new gal in town and sop up free beer.

Sunny served long necks to two cowboys playing pool. He eyed the shorts she had on and the way the white blouse only hinted at her shape as she moved about doing a little dance along the way, having fun but not exactly displaying a Reno showgirl's finesse. That amnesia had really done a number on her.

His insides burned as he watched her. What he wouldn't give to feel her in his arms again, like when she fallen against him practicing her dancing. He could almost feel her there now. Maybe she'd do it again.

'Course, that would be one very huge mistake. Sunny Kelly was all wrong for a guy running for mayor and wanting to prove to his brother he was a changed man. She was a rerun from his past…and then some. He should go, get away from her, stay away from temptation. *So why the hell didn't he?*

"What are you doing here?" she asked as she sauntered up to him.

That seemed to be the question of the night. He caught a whiff of her fresh scent and committed it to memory, no matter how much he shouldn't. "Looks like you know how to run a bar."

"Must be my showgirl background. I just sort of know what to do. And I like it." She glanced around. "I like the guys, but we could use some women in this place. Where are the women?"

"Home caring for the kids."

"Really. Hmm." Her lips drew into a thin line. "Seems like they need some fun, too. I think I need some flashier clothes."

"What's wrong with shorts? Tranquility isn't a sequin-and-feather kind of place. Shorts and a blouse are fine."

"Don't think I'll jump right to sequins. That's a little

too Reno. But red satin shorts and a white tank top would be nice. I think I was made to wear satin shorts, don't you?"

He ogled her long shapely legs. "No." He could picture Sunny in that outfit. *Holy cow.* "No fun. You're... the owner. Hell, owners aren't supposed to have fun. They're all business. Get a suit. Black. Pinstripes." He nodded at one of the servers. "What's Norm doing here?"

"Norm's a new employee. He said we survived the explosion together. He's a friend of Smitty's and Jean's and needs a job, and I'm definitely not wearing a suit. I hate suits. Showgirls spit on suits."

He didn't think she'd buy that last suggestion, but it had been worth a try. *Why the heck did he care, anyway?* "Norm used to work the rodeos till he got his leg caught in a gate. Have him make you one of his Dagwood sandwiches sometime."

Smitty, Jean and now Norm. Quite a crew. "Any idea how you're going to pay all these wages?"

She tossed her head and gave a sassy grin. "Bessy had some savings and I can get a second mortgage to fix things up, pay some wages, keep Six in things chewable and eat. If that doesn't work I'll think of something else. Showgirls are good at thinking on their feet."

She laughed. Did she have to do that—seem to be having the time of her life? Like all this was fresh and new and fun? How could he resist Sunny Kelly? "Where's Six?" he asked, not quite ready for her to leave.

She grinned at him. "Upstairs eating everything not nailed down. Total pain in the derriere."

He pushed his hat to the back of his head. "Heard somewhere a dog takes on the characteristics of its owner."

Her eyes danced. "I'll remember that."

"Also heard Ralph Nester turned your rodeo invitation down."

She arched her eyebrow and gave her head another toss. "That's not what I heard. I heard he's thinking it over and likes the idea and wants to call it Nester's Roundup. Kind of catchy."

"Nester doesn't know a cow from a rattlesnake." Tendrils of hair framed her face. No makeup, eyes bright. Downright gorgeous.

"We'll see about that." She strode away, picking up empties as she went. His gaze followed her as she took orders and filled them, talking, even laughing. His insides tightened. What could be so darn funny to make her laugh so much?

He headed for the bar and ordered a beer from Smitty…for old times' sake. He couldn't just walk out of The Smokehouse without one beer. Hell, the place would probably collapse if he tried such a thing. He said to Smitty, "See that guy in the corner, the one with the concrete truck on his shirt? Who is he?"

Smitty shook his head. "I have no idea. Just sitting there for the past hour or two, minding his own business."

Smitty sang along with Garth Brooks about having

friends in low places. When Gray turned back, the guy was gone, but he saw Sunny…this time by Widow Maker…and she was fending off Bad Boy Billy Barns.

He had her caged in his arms, holding hers straight. Gray stopped middrink. Something inside him snapped like a dry twig in August. He tore for Bad Billy, yanked him off Sunny and threw him across the room like a wet sock.

The bar went dead quiet. Surprise lit Bad Billy's face. "What the hell's wrong with you, McBride?"

Gray studied Billy and Sunny. She didn't seem hurt or scared of Billy. She *did* look royally pissed off at him. *Uh-oh*. He turned back to Billy. What had he missed? "Thought you were—"

Bad Billy was on his feet, his fist connecting with Gray's jaw, propelling him headfirst across a table. So much for thinking. When he landed on the other side, Billy's brother was there and his fist hit Gray's eye. He saw stars for a second, then jumped up and fended off another punch.

In the background Gray heard chairs crashing, tables overturning, glasses breaking, Sunny yelling, "Stop," and the unmistakable sound of his chances at being the next mayor of Tranquility going right down the toilet.

Out of the corner of an eye…his one good eye…he watched Sheriff Leroy and his deputy break up the ruckus in record time. Hell, they'd had enough practice at The Smokehouse. And twenty minutes later Gray wasn't surprised to be sharing a jail cell with the disheveled and none-too-happy proprietress of one slightly demolished saloon.

Sunny kicked the metal cot, kicked the wooden chair beside it, and Gray wouldn't have been surprised if she'd kicked him…only she didn't.

"I can't believe they arrest people for brawls in this town."

"The Smokehouse has a reputation and Sheriff Leroy is out of patience."

"How could you do this?" She pushed her hair from her face. "Is this your plan to get The Smokehouse closed down? And why are we locked in the same cell? Right now the sheriff should be considering your well-being because *I would love to beat you to a pulp.*"

Gray massaged his jaw. "I think the Barns brothers did the job for you."

"I have no desire to be anywhere near you." She glared at him. Least he thought it was a glare. Hard to tell with one eye completely swollen shut.

He sat on the cot and applied the ice pack Leroy had given him. Eye first or lip? "That lump in the second cell is Jimmy Smart. Jimmy doesn't play well with others. Sheriff knows I do my share of fighting, but I'm trustworthy, and I said I was sorry about all this and I meant it."

Her mouth pulled into a tight smile, but there was a twinkle in her eye. *Now what?*

"Sorry enough to help with the rodeo?"

"I only have so much sorrow. No one got hurt and

you heard me say this whole thing was my fault, so no one got arrested but me."

Her jaw dropped and she spread her arms wide. "What am I—the Ghost of Christmas Past? *I* got arrested."

"You're the owner. That's why you're in here with me. There's been tons of trouble at the saloon and Leroy wants it to stop. This is his way of showing you he means it. If you'd sold the bar in the first place like I told you to, you wouldn't be causing all this trouble and neither of us would be here."

"Me? *Me?* Did I throw that first punch?" She heaved a deep sigh and sat on the chair across from him. "So when do we get out?"

Gray stood and paced. Sitting so close to Sunny Kelly did strange things to his blood pressure. If he remembered correctly, the cell was five paces by six paces. "I just bet Leroy will tell his busybody wife what happened and by morning everyone will know about the fight. Those two are Tranquility's version of the local news, and me being in jail along with being connected to blowing up Lucky Tanner's gas station doesn't do much for my new image." He dropped his hat on the cot and raked his hair. "Fact is, since you showed up, my new-and-improved image has gone right to hell in a handbasket."

"Like my life is a bowl of cherries?"

Gray turned on the fifth pace and started back across the cell floor. "The judge will probably set the fine tomorrow morning."

Sunny jumped from the chair, missing him by inches and stopping him third stride. "I'm going to spend the night, the whole blasted night, in this jail with *you*? I've never been in jail before."

"How would you know?"

Her nose crinkled. "Some part of me would have remembered being in jail." She glanced around. "And I am not the one causing trouble here. You are! This is all your fault."

He paced in the other direction. "*You* have no business running a saloon. In Reno the casino owners look out for you. Who's doing that here? It was just a matter of time before some cowboy got his hands on you."

She blocked his path, their toes inches apart. "Nobody was getting his hands anywhere. Smitty and Norm were watching out for me. This was a wake. Everyone in that bar knew that. And we didn't even get to the sharing-stories-about-Bessy part."

"Least something good came out of this. Tell me, was Bad Billy taking care of you, too?"

"He was showing me how to brace my arms to ride that bull contraption, something about staying over your hands or getting tossed to the rafters. I asked him to show me. Everything was—"

"Well, why the hell didn't you ask me?" He froze. His lungs refused to work. He had no idea where that crack came from, but the words were out before he could stop them.

Her gaze fused with his like lightning to metal. Her

eyes darkened to forest green and she swallowed hard. Her lips parted and her teeth played with her bottom lip. "Ask…you?"

The only sound was his heart beating wildly. He carefully tucked a strand of hair behind her ear, his finger lingering a moment at her temple. Soft, delicate.

"Why does it matter who I ask?" she said in a quiet voice. His hand found her waist, the warmth of her skin seeping into his palm, their bodies inches…then an inch…apart.

"It…doesn't matter. It can't." He swallowed. "Forget it. Forget I asked." He released her and stepped away, his blood hot, his insides in a knot. He'd never forget the color of her eyes if he lived to be a million. How could she do this to him? He'd been around women plenty. He never lost his cool. *Till now in this damn jail cell.*

He started to pace again. He was jealous, dammit. Incredible as it seemed, he'd decked Billy because he was jealous over another man paying attention to Sunny, a woman he would never have a relationship with and who'd caused him more damn problems in the past three days than any other woman had caused in his whole damn life. And that was covering one hell of a lot of territory for Gray McBride.

He glanced at her, knowing he wanted to touch her again no matter how much trouble she caused him, and puffed out a deep breath. "It's going to be a long, long night," he said on a sigh.

He watched her hair glisten in the overhead light and

added two more *longs* to the length of this night. Then he nodded at the cot. "It's not the Hilton, but we better get some sleep. Judge Merryweather will be in court bright and early."

She looked from the cot to him. "Well, there's only one place to sleep. You got us in here, so I sleep." She handed him his hat. "You get the chair."

"Chair? Can't we share the cot? Divide it in half, top and bottom?" Better than a hard, metal chair. Gray watched Sunny lie down…the whole length…and try to snuggle into the lumpy mattress. And to think he'd been feeling jealous about her. Forget her. Now all he wanted was that cot.

"Accommodations aren't great, but they seem clean enough." She closed her eyes.

He pulled the chair over, sat down and propped his feet on the edge of the metal frame, then slid his hat over his eyes, keeping the ice in place and blocking out the light—though with the holes, that was more theory than reality.

"I need a pillow."

"Concierge desk is closed. Ran out of strawberries and champagne. Go to sleep." He listened to her toss and turn and grumble, then settle down. His eye throbbed, his jaw ached, but he was tired to the bone and started to doze off, only to be jarred awake again by more tossing and turning and grumbling.

"Dang, woman!" He stood, lifted her head, sat down and set her head on his thigh. "There. You got your blasted pillow." And he got a softer seat.

He shouldn't do this. He needed to stay away from her. But he had to get some rest!

And who the hell was he kidding? He *wanted* to be close to Sunny, no matter how much he shouldn't. This could very well be the last time he'd ever be able to get this close to her.

He leaned back against the concrete-block wall, savoring the feel of her cheek on his leg, her breath seeping through his jeans to his skin. He put his hat back over his eyes, then said, "Go to sleep."

SLEEP? YEAH, RIGHT! With the steel-hard muscles of Gray's leg against her cheek. And the smooth, well-worn denim of his jeans reminding her just how male Gray McBride really was. *Like she needed reminding.* How in blazes was she supposed to sleep when she was so close to Gray?

"You're not sleeping. Miss your silk sheets?"

"Not exactly. I miss…Six."

She felt Gray's leg muscles tighten, then relax as he settled. All this movement, compounded by her proximity to him, did not help her present lustful condition. "I'm sure Smitty will take care of Six till I get out of here. Six is good company. Nights are lonely. Guess it's the amnesia. That dog does a lot to fill up the space."

"Hmm."

"He's got his eye on a pretty white poodle in pink bows and a jewel collar."

"That would be Lucky Tanner's Mimi, his pride and joy, and since it was Lucky's gas station that you blew to hell and back, I suggest you tell Six to do his courting elsewhere before he gets a back end full of buckshot."

"That *I* blew to hell and back?" She started to sit, to confront Gray eye to eye, until he pushed her head back onto his leg.

"How can you sleep, McBride?"

"I can't because somebody keeps yammering at me like a broken record!"

She listened to his breathing slow and felt the muscles in his leg relax once more. She'd never met a man like him. Then again, how did she know if she'd met someone like him or not? Maybe she'd met a hundred men like Gray McBride. Truth be told, she doubted if there *were* a hundred men like Gray. Not only was he sexy and handsome, but family came first. He belonged to them and took their welfare seriously, above his own pleasure and what *he* wanted. And he was willing to change his life to take care of them. Gray McBride, family man, protector, basic do-gooder and from all accounts, a really fine cowboy.

Nope, she'd remember someone like Gray no matter how many times she got whacked in the head. But what she had to figure out now was how to focus some of his commendable behavior her way. She needed his help on the rodeo. She needed to keep The Smokehouse open not only for herself but for Smitty, Jean and their baby and Six and now Norm. If she lost the place, where would they all go?

She'd taken them in and now they were her respon-

sibility. She had to come up with something. That was
what Auntie would have done, Sunny was sure of it.

How was she going to pull it off, though? She'd
bluffed about Nester's help with the rodeo. Actually,
she'd out and out lied, because Nester had turned her
down flat. Somehow, she had to persuade Gray to
change his mind. Take a chance. And that was her last
thought till Sheriff Leroy unlocked the jail the next
morning and handed her and Gray a cup of coffee. Then
the sheriff ushered them into Merryweather's courtroom.

Chapter Three

As Sunny stood beside Gray in the courtroom, she wondered how in the world he could spend the night in jail and still look so handsome. The swollen eye gave him a dangerous, male appearance. Early-morning stubble should make him grubby, right? *Wrong.* More like sexy and rugged. Her gaze dropped to his chest. Broad. Cowboy broad. She sucked in a quick breath.

"Ms. Kelly," Judge Merryweather barked.

"Yes." She jumped. Was that pathetic squeak really hers? The judge squinted his eyes, his glasses riding low on his nose, his gray hair on end, as if he'd gotten too close to the ceiling fan. "Are you all right?"

"Yes, Your Honor." She swallowed. "Peachy, Your Honor."

Judge Merryweather cleared his throat as he studied the papers in front of him. "Says here you've only been in town three days." His gaze rolled up to meet hers. "And already you've been a guest in our jail for the night? This does not bode well for you or your business, Ms. Kelly."

She saw Gray open his mouth to say something, but since it was her saloon, she needed to defend it. "Your Honor, I'm making changes to The Smokehouse. Giving it a new image. There will be no more fighting. This won't happen again. I guarantee it."

"I don't know how you intend to do that, but the town and I will hold you to it. Since this is your first offense, you get off with a warning not to be back here again."

He stared at Gray, his eyes narrowing, his forehead creasing. "Mr. McBride, you on the other hand, have been in my jail more times than I have fingers. Fighting in a saloon and spending the night in jail are not proper behavior for a potential mayor." He shook his head. "And—"

"Your Honor," Sunny interrupted in a burst of inspiration. "Mr. McBride was at The Smokehouse to pay his respects to my poor deceased auntie and to discuss the rodeo the Lazy K and The Smokehouse are putting on for the town during the Fourth of July celebration. He merely got caught up in a fight that broke out."

Merryweather stroked his chin and leaned back in his chair. "Rodeo?"

"That's why Gray was at the bar. We were discussing it."

"Well, now. That does shed new light on things, being it's about a rodeo and all. This town sure does love a good rodeo and it's a shame we don't have one regular like."

She gave Merryweather a huge grin and spread her

arms wide. "What a coincidence! That's exactly what Gray said. Tranquility should have an annual rodeo. And he took the rap so no one else there would have to go to jail. Very honorable, don't you agree?"

Gray's eyes widened, his lips moving but nothing coming out. He found his voice and said, "Judge, I don't know what Ms. Kelly is—"

"Your Honor," Sunny stated. "May I confer with Mr. McBride for a moment? He's not feeling well, being the victim and all."

"Victim?" The judge's bushy eyebrows shot up. "Gray McBride?" Merryweather shook his head. "Oh, very well, but only because there's a rodeo involved."

Sunny turned to Gray as he whispered, "What are you doing? You're lying to a judge."

"Shh. I'm stretching the truth to a judge. *Reader's Digest* said it was okay…least, I think it was *Reader's Digest*. Anyway, I'm making *you* into a hero."

"I'm not helping with any rodeo."

She narrowed her eyes a fraction. "If you want to be mayor you will. Look at Merryweather up there." She glanced at the front of the courtroom, grinned and gave a little finger wave. "He's all atwitter about the rodeo. He thinks you were at the bar to set up a rodeo and took the fall to save others. If he keeps me here long enough I can get a statue of you erected in the town's square before noon. *I'm on a roll.*"

"What about the firehouse?"

"If the rodeo is a big enough success you can build a new firehouse, just like I said. Add it to the money you were going to use to buy me out and, bingo, new firehouse."

The judge interrupted. "Ms. Kelly, this here court does not have all day. It has a tee-off time at ten o'clock, if you get my drift. I suggest you two get your rodeo problems hammered out later."

Gray whispered again, "I want the saloon closed. It's part of my campaign."

"I'll change the saloon. Make it better. I just rescued your chance at the election. Saved you from being a troublemaker with the town *and* your brother. Now, tell the nice judge about the rodeo and let's get to work making you the next mayor and saving my saloon."

And twenty minutes later, Sunny followed Gray out the main entrance of the courthouse, tickled to her toes her plan had worked. 'Course, she'd sort of dragged Gray into this plan kicking and fighting, but he did come. She faced the sky and held her arms up, taking it in. "Ah, freedom."

Gray pulled up beside her and stuck his hands into his pockets. "What the hell have you gotten me into? You should be a lawyer."

"Me? Never. I like being a showgirl-slash-saloon-keeper. Kind of footloose and fancy free." She did a little dance on the sidewalk, but it felt…clumsy. "What I did there was save your backside. This will all work out great."

He stood in front of her, readjusted his hat, then cupped her chin in his palm, tipping her face to his. His hand made her warm all over; his deep brown eyes fascinated her. She hadn't expected him to touch her.

He said, "If I don't continue to push for closing The Smokehouse not only will we not have a big enough firehouse, but everyone will now think I've fallen for another beautiful, wild sexy woman who also owns a saloon and happens to be a Reno showgirl. My new reputation as settled and responsible will be shot to hell and I wouldn't get elected dogcatcher around here."

"B-beautiful? Sexy? Did you just say I was beautiful and sexy?"

"Of course you're…"

The whole world seemed to stand still for a split second—the people on the sidewalk, the traffic on the street, the droplets in the fountain. She shivered, then boiled. She wanted to be in his arms the way she'd been when she'd missed those dance steps and he'd held her close.

How could this happen? How could she be so attracted to someone so off-limits? Gray was right. She was completely the wrong woman for him and she had to end her attraction to him before it got any worse. She owed him that since she'd just bamboozled him into helping with the rodeo.

She took a step away, pulled in a deep breath and called herself every name referring to *idiot* for what she was about to do. "Just because you're helping with the rodeo and The Smokehouse stays open, no one in town will think you've fallen for another unsettled woman—" her insides wept "—because I'll find you the perfect responsible girlfriend."

"A what?"

She stiffened her spine and snagged his sleeve, making him walk with her. She couldn't carry out her plan if she continued to gaze into his scrumptious brown eyes and study his handsome face, with that little chin scar hidden in early-morning stubble. What woman could resist that for more than two minutes? *Not her!*

"*Girlfriend.* You know, those people who smell yummy and leave their lipstick on your collar…and other places. I'll find you someone your family will like and the town will adore, someone who'll help you get elected."

And act as a buffer between you and me. If Gray had another woman on his arm, Sunny would lose interest in him. She was sure of it.

They paused at the crosswalk and he said, "I'll get elected if I turn The Smokehouse into a fire department like I planned. It's a sure thing. And I can find my own girlfriends."

"You're already committed to the rodeo, unless you want to back out and upset Merryweather and the whole town. Everyone's talking about it by now. It's been twenty-five minutes since we were in the courthouse, enough time for gossip to spread everywhere."

She touched his arm, her fingers lingering a moment. "I'll find a girlfriend for you with political ties who knows about campaigns and Texas."

"You're setting me up with George Bush, right?"

They stopped by his pickup and she adjusted his collar, which had turned with the breeze. She was so tired and all she wanted to do was cuddle into his strong arms and sleep. Well, maybe not just sleep. A little kissing would be nice. But there would be no cuddling, no sleeping, no kissing. She had to find someone for Gray and do it fast. Then she'd immerse herself in fixing up The Smokehouse, taking care of Smitty, Norm and Six and *forget about Gray*. Heck, when would she have time to think about Gray? Wasn't that the way she wanted things to be until she got her memory back? No time to brood, no time to think. Just work.

He climbed into the truck as she said, "Well, cowboy, it's been an interesting night. You sure can show a girl a good time. I'll call you later and let you know what I come up with."

He cranked the engine and shook his head. "This has disaster written all over it."

"Trust me."

"Oh, boy."

BY THE NEXT AFTERNOON, as Gray drove into town after Sunny called, he was more convinced than ever that any plan she had to help him was totally doomed. *Her* find *him* a girlfriend—*good grief!* He was going to tell her today that all bets were off. He'd get elected by himself, campaign for closing the saloon and run his own campaign. The saloon was history and…and he had no idea what he'd say to Merryweather about the rodeo.

He parked the pickup, got out and spied a poster advertising the upcoming rodeo with his name as contact person. She was one fast worker. How would he get out of the rodeo now? Score one for Sunny Kelly. She'd outsmarted him this time. He studied The Smokehouse...least, he thought it was The Smokehouse. Hard to recognize the place with the front porch gone, and Smitty and Norm and now Art were swarming around it.

"Hey, Gray McBride. Up here," came Sunny's voice. She sat cross-legged on the roof, waving a hammer. "Climb up and join me."

He stepped back to get a better look. Keeping track of Sunny Kelly was like keeping track of a leaf in a tornado. He smiled in spite of being hoodwinked into the rodeo.

She waved again and grinned back. He could almost feel her enthusiasm. She was that way about everything she did; never anything halfway with Sunny Kelly.

She yelled, "I'm putting on shingles. Want to finish before the rain." She jabbed her hammer toward the gathering clouds overhead. "Watch."

She swung her hammer and from the sounds of it, it missed the nail more than hit. She glanced up, a triumphant expression on her face. "I got news. Ladder's around back."

He made his way to the roof, which really did need new shingles. Place must leak like a rusty tin can. He followed the hammering, up one side of the peak, then down the other. He sat beside her. "Okay. What's the news that can't wait?"

Her baggy white T-shirt was stained, her face sunburned and smeared with sweat and dirt, and her hair was damp and clinging. Putting shingles on a roof under the Texas sun was exhausting, he knew that from experience. The few overhanging trees offered some shade but not much. The clouds just made things humid as hell. "You shouldn't be doing this. And when did you take on Art?"

"Today. He used to be a cowboy till arthritis set in. Figure he can help with the rodeo. The three of them are doing the heavy stuff and I can do this. The man at the hardware store said putting on a roof was a piece of cake."

Gray studied the mangled nail and was about to take exception to her statement but didn't. She'd tried. She'd tried really hard. Must have taken her ten strokes to accomplish what he could do in one. Tomorrow he'd have a little chat with the guys at the hardware store. They should never have talked Sunny into such a big project…and they'd better not try to make a sale that way again. Some older person could have a heart attack. Tranquility was better than that. People here watched out for one another.

Sunny pushed her hair from her face with the back of her gloved hand, leaving another dirty smear. She smiled, but this time the smile didn't quite reach her eyes. She was exhausted. If he had five workers like her on the Lazy K he'd be a lucky man. Once again, he found himself admiring her, and he wasn't in the habit of admiring all that many people. He kissed her on the forehead, feeling the heat of her skin on his lips and tasting the salty perspiration.

She stared at him wide-eyed.

"You looked like someone who needed a kiss." Truth be told, he had no idea why he'd kissed her, other than the fact he'd wanted to. He took off his neckerchief and wiped her face. He took off his hat and put it on her head. "Keep the sun out of your eyes."

She studied him for a moment. "Cowboys never give away their hats, even their old ones. Least, that's what I hear."

He winked. "Especially their old ones, and they only give them away to stop someone from keeling over with sunstroke. It's the cowboy way. Besides, it's just on loan."

Did she have to be so damn cute, even sweaty and dirty and wearing oversize work gloves?

"Uh, well...thanks. I've...I've got a woman for you."

He shook his head. He couldn't even think of another woman besides Sunny right now. "This isn't a great idea. Let's call it off." He started to get up and she yanked him back down.

"It *is* a great idea. What do you have to lose? Just going out with this woman I've picked out for you ups your respectability quotient. You might go out with her again, propose, get married and have ten kids."

"I haven't gone on the first date yet! Give me a break."

"I can't help it if I'm the optimistic sort." Sunny nailed a shingle in place. Least, she tried to. Her eye-hand coordination sucked. How could a dancer have such bad dexterity? Residual effects of the blast, no doubt.

"The woman I have in mind will not only help you win the election, but your brother will love her, your entire family will love her, your cattle will really love her." Sunny smiled. "This perfect woman is Maggie Winslow."

"The vet?" Gray felt his eyes roll around in his head. "She...she must be forty."

"Thirty-five. And her father and two uncles are on city council and her mother is chairwoman of the historical society. Why didn't you ask this woman out before?"

"She's six years older than me. I think she even baby-sat me once or twice. *I can't date my babysitter.*"

"She's not baby-sitting anymore and she's just what you need." Sunny snagged a plastic water bottle and took a long drink, holding his hat on as she tipped back her head. Water moistened her lips. A few drops trickled down the side of her mouth and over her throat, leaving clean wet paths. His gaze followed the drops till they disappeared under her T-shirt.

He burned! It had nothing to do with sitting on a hot roof or dating Maggie Winslow, and everything to do with a few drops of water and where they went. "I...I don't want to go out with Maggie Winslow."

Sunny offered him the bottle and he took a long drink. Something had to cool him off. Then he thought of his lips being where Sunny's were and he didn't cool off one degree. He felt hotter.

"Sure you want to date Maggie." Sunny selected a nail and pummeled it. "In fact, you've got a dinner date with her tonight at seven over at the Mill Pond Restaurant. And the reason I'm telling you now and not over the phone is that I knew you'd refuse and now you're here and can't get out of it."

"Wanna bet?" He jumped up, spilling the water and nearly sliding off the roof.

"You're making a scene. Everyone's staring." She nodded at the workmen and people on the sidewalk.

He smiled, waved, then sat back down. "You want to tell me how you got the town vet to date me? I never thought she even liked me. Gray nodded at a stranger he'd noticed on the street corner. See that guy down there, the one in the baseball cap with a cement-truck logo? Do you know him? He seems to be hanging around here a lot."

"I don't know anyone. I have amnesia. I'm the town curiosity. Maybe he wants to sell me concrete to fix up the saloon." She gave Gray a confused look. "Though I do have the feeling I know something about him."

"But you just got here."

She shrugged. "You're right. He's nothing to me. And you're also right about Maggie not liking you. I met her when I brought Six in for a checkup. Smitty said she's great and he's right. Anyway, I walked in her office and there she was, all happy and perky, and she told me about her family. So this morning when Six and I stopped by her office for a doggie snack I told her how you've changed. How you saved me and befriended me because of the amnesia and all. That you took in strays and gave me Six. She liked that a lot. I said I knew for a fact you admired her from afar and would love to have a date with her but were too shy to ask her."

"And she bought it?" He watched the stranger walk on. What was up with that guy? Gray handed Sunny another shingle.

"The shy part was a tough sell, but I'm a showgirl from Reno. Illusion is my business. I told her you were charming under all that ego."

"What ego?"

"She'll be waiting at seven. And if this doesn't work out I've got my eye on Susie Longford over at the furniture store. Her father's the middle-school principal and—"

"I know who he is. I don't want to get fixed up with all these women. I don't like others running my life. And how did you get to know all these people?"

"Smitty, of course. He knows everyone." Sunny pointed the hammer at him. "And you're the one who wants to be mayor and win over your brother's trust, so quit your griping. One of these women is just what you need. There's a whole other world of responsible women for you, Gray. Connected women, sensible women, extremely capable women, women who can take a loaf of bread and stick of butter and serve up a ten-course dinner for fifty in twenty minutes. You'll fall head over heels in love if you give them a chance. What more could you ask for?"

"A little fun. A little excitement. Pizzazz."

She patted his hand with her gloved one. "Pizzazz is in the past, cowboy. Think *mayor*. Maybe Maggie will have pizzazz if you give her a chance."

He liked Sunny's hand on his. He eyed her long tanned legs and groaned aloud.

"It's not that bad. You'll get used to the staid life. It takes practice." She whacked at another shingle, then handed him a hammer. "Help me fix the rest of these shingles and I'll go shopping with you to buy some new clothes."

"I already have clothes, and there's no way in this world you're going to persuade me to work on this saloon unless I'm connecting it to the firehouse right back there." He pointed over his shoulder.

"I bet you don't have the right kind of clothes. Bet you have nothing but cowboy clothes, jeans and stuff."

"I only wear suits to weddings and funerals." He pulled his work gloves from his back pocket.

"If you want to get elected mayor, you're wearing a suit. It can be western cut."

"Gee, thanks."

"But something nice, conservative, blue-gray, and you can think of this date as a funeral of your old life." She grinned.

He scowled as he put on the gloves, picked up a shingle and hammered it in place.

She said, "This town's not going to elect some cowboy who looks like he should be roping little doggies.

They want a mayor who appears responsible and can represent the town. A suit will make you seem older. Maybe I should put silver streaks at your temples."

"No!"

She handed him another shingle. "All right, all right. No silver."

He gave her a sideways glance. "Where do you get all this energy?"

"Hey, I'm a showgirl. Always on the go. And it keeps my mind off the amnesia. Even though I'm staying here till I get my other life back, I still wonder about it sometimes, and that does no good at all."

Damn. He'd forgotten what she must be going through, not knowing anything or anyone. He admired her for coping as well as she did. 'Course, he also wanted to wring her pretty little neck for messing up his campaign.

"The shops close at five. You can change at my place. I'm staying in Bessy's apartment right under this roof. Bessy lived kind of sparse, not a lot of stuff around. There won't be time for you to run back to the Lazy K and get back to town by seven. Besides, you need my input. Before you leave on that date you're going to look like *GQ* goes western."

"I came here to tell you I'm not doing the rodeo."

"I've already made up flyers for registration and contacted some of the civic clubs."

He set his mouth in a firm line and glared at her.

"Okay, okay. We'll talk about the rodeo later. Let's just concentrate on Maggie for now."

He grabbed a handful of nails. "I'll get Dillon for this. If it's the last thing I do."

"You have to be elected mayor first."

Then she laughed, making him feel good all over. How'd she do that? How could he come here determined to call this whole idiotic idea off and end up planning to go on a blind date and putting a roof on The Smokehouse?

Because some part of him wanted to please Sunny Kelly and make her laugh the way she just did. And he had no idea at all why…other than the fact that it made him happy, too.

"GRAY," SUNNY YELLED through the closed bathroom door in her apartment. "Have you fallen asleep in that shower or what? Did I hear snoring? It's almost six-thirty. You'll be late. I've got a feeling Maggie Winslow is never late."

The water stopped. "I'll make it, and I do not snore."

"Yeah, that's what all guys say."

His voice was hollow, echoing off the tile and porcelain. "Maggie isn't my type at all, you know. This is crazy. It's never going to work."

"Maggie's cute."

"She reminds me of a poodle, with all those curls."

"Poodles are cute…and smart."

"And yappy. Very yappy. I hate yappy."

"There are new disposable razors and shaving cream on the shelf over the tub. I'm going into the kitchen. You can have my bedroom all to yourself to get beautified. But *hurry*."

She could hear more water running and Gray moving about. She imagined him maneuvering in the tiny space, bending down for the shower, the sink, to see himself in the mirror. She imagined him muscled from hard work, deliciously tanned from being outdoors, and she imagined him buck naked.

Where'd that come from? From the night in jail coupled with that kiss on the roof, that was where. Gray might have intended the kiss as a friendly gesture, but it had ended up more, lots more. She could just imagine his six-pack abs, trim waist, tight butt. Her insides boiled and her throat went dry.

The water running in the bathroom suddenly stopped. She had to get out of here. Gray would open the door any second and probably be bare or pretty darn near it. She headed for the doorway to the hall, turned back in a moment of driving lust, wanting nothing more than to see if her image of Gray was right. *What was wrong with her? She couldn't do that. Could she? No!*

She turned again and left, tripping over Six in the hallway, stumbling into the wall. Did salivating over Gray McBride have to be so dangerous and so painful? "Sorry, Six."

He opened one eye, gave her a *what's wrong with you* look, then fell back to sleep. She snagged the bedroom door shut and went into the sitting room, searching for something to get her mind off the hot, sexy, unclothed man in her bedroom. Unless an earthquake occurred, that wasn't going to happen.

She lit the little blue ceramic lamp on the desk and zeroed in on the Bible. She opened it and located her name on the family tree at the front. Every name had a birth date and death date but hers. *Sunny Kelly, Reno.* She really was Bessy's only living relative.

Sunny gazed out the window, catching her reflection in the glass. One of these days she'd remember. Or, maybe one of these days someone would come for her.

"Sunny?"

She spun around to face Gray, her heart beating wildly. "You scared the life out of me."

"You were a million miles away." He eyed the Bible. "Anything come to mind?"

"Yeah, I'm not dead." She took in the way the sport coat fit him perfectly. The way the blue in the shirt brought out his dark eyes. Yeah, a lot came to mind. That he was the most attractive man on earth, with or without clothes. "The sport coat seems to fit well."

He stretched out his arms, peering at the material. "I've never worn a blue dress shirt. Do I look like a complete dork?"

"Maggie Winslow will probably jump your bones and have mad passionate sex with you in the middle of the Mill Pond Restaurant!"

He froze. His eyes shot wide-open.

"I'm kidding." *Ha!* "Just trying to lighten things up. You look terrific. And you're right about not needing a tie. You don't need anything." *But I need a cold shower.*

She regrouped her thoughts. "Talk to Maggie about what plans you have for the town. She'll like that."

He glanced at his watch. "I better get a move on."

"Wait." She went into the bedroom and returned with his hat. She dusted it, pushed the material tighter around the holes and handed it to him. "You don't go anywhere without your hat."

He flashed a killer smile, the kind guaranteed to melt any woman into a blob. She was living proof. He slid on the hat, then rested his hands on her shoulders. "I know you did this as part of your plan for saving your precious saloon, but thanks for all your efforts, anyway." He smooched her a kiss right on the mouth. A noisy friendly kiss for fun. Between friends. Then jerked back.

He winked, or at least he tried to. He seemed…confused. He said, "That…that was for…luck. Maybe your idea will work."

Before she could catch her breath he was out the door, his boots beating a retreat down the outside wooden steps.

Luck? That kiss was not lucky. It was what she'd wanted to steer clear of. She slowly licked her lips, savoring the taste of Gray. She could still feel the pressure of his mouth on hers and the warmth of his hard, strong body next to hers. She sat down in the wicker rocker, missed and plopped right down onto the wooden floor. How could one friendly little kiss throw her off balance?

Did Maggie Winslow have any idea at all what kind

of man Gray McBride was? How incredibly handsome? How sexy? How responsible and kindhearted. Would she appreciate him? Yeah, any woman would appreciate the likes of Gray McBride.

Okay, this was good. Not her obsessing over him, but the fact that her plan would probably work. Maggie Winslow was a fine person; everyone in town and Gray's family would approve of her in a heartbeat. Gray would fall for her; Sunny was sure of that, too. Well…mostly she was sure. Maybe she should go to the Mill Pond in case things didn't work out. Then she could see what went wrong and avoid it if she had to set Gray up with someone else.

She *had* to get Gray hooked up with a woman. Get him out of her life and her brain as fast as she could, because the longer he was unattached the more she felt herself falling for him. That couldn't happen, so she had to come up with plan B to fall back on in case something went wrong tonight.

She found Elizabeth McBride's business card and picked up the phone. She'd wanted to thank her for helping with Bessy's will, and dinner tonight at the Mill Pond was the perfect answer. And a half hour later she sat across from Elizabeth at a little table at the back of the restaurant behind a row of bushy silk atmosphere-enhancing cattails.

Elizabeth sipped orange juice, ordered beef Wellington, then changed to soup and crackers and asked Sunny, "So how's The Smokehouse coming along? I hear you're keeping it open."

Sunny peeked between two cattails. Maggie and Gray were at a table in the far corner, by a window overlooking the pond. Very romantic, just as Sunny had requested.

"Expecting someone else?"

Sunny pushed the cattails back together and grinned at Elizabeth. "Uh, The Smokehouse needs a lot of work. Just what you'd expect. But I'm trying to turn it around. Who's minding the twins?"

"Dillon."

"Wow. How'd that happen?"

"He's expecting a business call at nine. But I have to be home by then, because when he's tied up with work he forgets anything else exists, including twin boys."

Sunny smiled at Elizabeth and once again gently elbowed apart the plants, catching a glimpse of Maggie's dark brown hair glistening in the low light. She wore a blue silk dress—the same shade as Gray's shirt. No lab coat stained with doggie and cat drool tonight.

Elizabeth said, "My goodness, it's Gray, with Maggie Winslow."

Sunny glanced over and realized Elizabeth was peering through another bunch of cattails. She eyed Sunny and arched an eyebrow. "I wondered what was so interesting out there. We should go say hello to Gray."

"Let's not." Sunny swallowed and they both pushed the cattails together. Sunny puffed out a breath of air and sipped her water. "I sort of fixed him up with Maggie."

"Good heavens, why? I mean, Gray's never been hard up for dates."

Sunny rested her arms on the table, then leaned forward. "Gray should find a responsible, settled woman. It will help with his mayoral campaign, show the townspeople he's a changed man, and Dillon will acknowledge Gray's astute decision-making abilities and give him added responsibility."

"Sometimes you really don't sound like a showgirl."

"It's the *Reader's Digest*. Anyway, I think Maggie and Gray are well suited. He has a lot of cattle—she's a vet." They both like dogs. Sunny nodded at the cattails. "They do make a handsome couple."

"If you squeeze your water glass any tighter your fingerprints will be permanently embossed."

Sunny put down the glass and forced a grin. "Tell me about the twins."

Gray chuckled. She could pick it out clear across the room. Not that he was loud, but she just…*knew*. She scooted to the side of her chair and tilted her head. She could see between the reeds without even moving them. Pretty slick.

"The twins are fine. I feed them bananas and they swing from the chandeliers by their tails. Then we put them in their cages."

"You're such a good mother."

Elizabeth laughed. "Oh, honey, you've got it bad. One of the worst cases I've ever seen."

Sunny snapped her head around and Elizabeth

leaned back in her chair. "I better warn you, in a few minutes the piano player, Joey Wilson, comes on and people dance. That means Gray's hands will be on Maggie, and Maggie's hands on Gray. Think you can handle it?"

Sunny huffed, "This is what's supposed to happen. Just what I planned. A wonderful date between two people who will..." Her gaze connected with Elizabeth's and all her courage and stamina and pseudohappiness vanished, replaced by a big knot in her stomach. Gray chuckled again and Sunny's insides dissolved into a puddle. "I...I have to go."

She stood, fished some money from her pocket and dropped it on the table. "I can't do this. I'm...I'm just not feeling well. I'm so sorry to ruin your night out, but...but..." She let out a deep breath. "I don't know what's wrong with me. I just feel...terrible."

Elizabeth shook her head and smiled. "You didn't ruin anything. Seeing two people fall in love is always exciting."

Sunny tipped her chin toward Maggie and Gray. "They really do make a nice couple."

Elizabeth's grin grew and her eyes danced. "I wasn't talking about *Maggie* and Gray." She patted Sunny's hand as she started to leave and held it for just a second. "The McBride men are a breed apart, Sunny. Stubborn and ornery. 'Course, they're also courageous, honorable, dependable and damn terrific lovers."

Sunny felt heat rush to her cheeks. "I...I don't see what this has to do with me."

Elizabeth grinned. "Oh, you will." She chuckled. "Just wait."

Chapter Four

Gray left the Mill Pond Restaurant and headed down Oak Street. He shed his jacket and flipped it over his shoulder as a gentle evening breeze rolled through Tranquility; crickets and frogs joined in a summer duet and three Vote For Nester posters stared at him from across the street. The election was heating up and Gray was not on the front burner.

The date with Maggie, planned to help his situation, hadn't done diddly. After he realized *No match in heaven here,* he'd introduced her to the piano player, Joey Wilson. How could two people live in the same town, day after day and not realize they were perfect for each other? Gray McBride, resident matchmaker. Too bad that didn't make him resident mayor.

He walked toward The Smokehouse, needing to pick up his clothes and see Sunny. He'd missed her a hell of a lot more than he should have tonight. All through dinner he'd thought about her, could almost feel her presence, as though she was right there with him. Fallout from the kiss, the one he'd planted on her when he'd left, the one he hadn't planned on but that had nearly singed his eyebrows. How could a simple lip-to-lip, walk-by kiss do that?

Fixing up Maggie with another guy, kissing Sunny, hanging out at The Smokehouse and getting tossed in jail didn't make for great election strategy…unless you happened to be the opponent. Gray's recent screwups must thrill Nester to his toes.

When Gray reached the saloon, lights shone through the windows downstairs, silhouetting Sheriff Leroy ambling down the rickety front steps, the only part of the porch left. Gray waited till Leroy rounded the next corner before crossing the street. Nester had enough ammunition against Gray already without adding his associating with Sunny to it. He gritted his teeth. He hated this. He went where he wanted, associated with whomever he pleased…except now, when he needed to win this damn election. He pushed open the red paint-chipped door, which sported a Closed For Repairs sign, and went in.

Cans, rags, ladders and mops cluttered a corner of the room still in need of TLC; a sheet covered the pool table, another covered Widow Maker and the mats. Fresh varnish gave old tables, chairs and stools a warm welcoming glow. The mirror sparkled, overhead lights gleamed. *Well, dang!* He had no idea The Smokehouse could look so good.

Smitty held his position behind the bar now littered with booze bottles. Jean, Norm, Art, Doc and Sunny occupied stools. The guys had beers, Jean a teacup and

Sunny an empty glass. Everyone but Sunny nodded *howdy* as Six pranced over to Gray and parked on his left foot. He scratched Six behind the ears. "What did Leroy want?"

Smitty rolled his shoulders. "Snooping around. He's as nosy as that wife of his. Asked if we'd seen a woman here, asking about The Smokehouse. Someone's trying to get ahold of her."

Gray wagged his head. "Don't tell me someone else wants to buy this place? Why?"

Doc bit into a sandwich. "How was your date?" he asked around a mouthful.

Gray's toes numbed as Six nuzzled his leg, begging for attention. The dog must have put on five pounds since Sunny had taken him. "How'd you know about my date?"

"Hell, it's been two hours, Gray. Whole town's talking. You had blueberry cobbler for desert, Maggie's singing show tunes with Joey Wilson and you left alone, looking pleased as punch. What kind of date is that?"

Six wandered back to his spot in the corner and Gray laid his jacket across a chair. He flexed his toes to restart the circulation and waited for Sunny to turn around and have a conniption over his not falling madly in love with the woman who'd get him elected mayor. But Sunny kept her back to him and didn't budge, as though glued in place.

Hmm. It wasn't like her to let things slide without some sassy comment, or to stay in one place for more

than a few seconds. She was a perpetual-motion ma-
chine. He caught her reflection in the mirror. She
seemed mesmerized by the brown liquor bottles in
front of her, as if they held all the answers to life. Or
maybe she was just zonked. "What's she drinking?"

Norm sighed. "You name it—she's drinking it."

Her gaze collided with his in the mirror. Frustration
he'd felt all evening from being with Maggie and not
Sunny pummeled him like a charging bull, making his
body react in ways it shouldn't in public. Casually he
made his way around the bar to the back to hide his ob-
vious condition. "Is Sunny okay?"

He wasn't. He was losing his mind and his self-con-
trol. He never had this problem before. *Dang.*

Smitty folded his arms. "Been acting mighty strange
all evening, like something's on her mind that she
didn't want to be there, and she's chasing it away with
the help of the booze. She really hasn't had that much.
More *what* she's had and how she's putting it together."
Smitty made a face as though he'd just swallowed lava.

- Norm sipped from a long neck and offered Gray
one. "She thinks The Smokehouse needs one of those
signature drinks. You know, one that goes with the bar."

Gray shoved his hat to the back of his head. "It's a
cowboy bar. Cowboys don't want little umbrellas in
their beer. We're easy. Toss us a bottle opener."

Doc shook his head, knocking his toupee a bit left.
"Sunny says Trader Vic's has the Hurricane, the Rain-
bow Room has its Golden Cadillac. The Smokehouse
should have—"

"What?" said Gray. "Fireworks?"

Sunny slammed her palm flat on the bar, making the bottles jump and glasses rattle. "That's it." She swiveled on the stool and faced him. "The Fireworks. Besides cowboys, firefighters will hang out here, too. Heck, they're right behind us. This will improve our horizontal analysis."

Norm's forehead knit into one shaggy line. "What'd she say?"

Doc claimed another bit of sandwich and mumbled, "It's a *Reader's Digest* thing."

Sunny poured bourbon into a glass and added lime juice, Coke and an olive. She held it high. "The Fireworks."

"Try Belly Bomb." Gray's stomach rolled and his lips curled as she gulped. He asked Doc, "You're here to pick up the pieces?"

"Came over to see how she's getting on. Thought I'd hang around a bit when I saw the bottles."

"And mooch a sandwich," added Norm. "I fixed him my best Dagwood."

Doc bit a pickle in half. Sunny belched and studied the glass. "Lacking something. Tabasco sauce. And a pickle." She snagged Doc's other half and dropped it in the glass.

Norm and Art groaned, Jean turned green and Gray said to Doc, "Ms. Rose is going to be madder than a flattened hornet's nest if you're too full to eat the dinner she left for you."

Sunny added Tabasco along with tequila and an or-

ange slice and sipped. Gray searched for a bottle of
Pepto-Bismol and Doc stroked his chin and said, "Ms.
Rose is on a vacation. Off to see her sister over in Dry
Run."

A scowl crept across his face. "Dang-blasted
woman. What am I supposed to do while she's gone?
Tell me that. Starve to death? Don't know what she did
with my new reading glasses." He slid his old glasses
from his pocket. "Look here. These are held together
with a kiddy Band-Aid."

Sunny swiped the back of her hand across her mouth
as she studied the bottles, and Smitty said, "Don't ever
remember Ms. Rose taking a vacation with all her
women committees. Bet they're in a state without her."

Sunny hiccuped. "Seems the women do an awful lot
of the volunteer work around here, and the men do a
lot of bowling and card playing and swaggering." She
mixed tequila, Coke and rum and asked Doc, "What'd
you say to Ms. Rose to get 'er upset?"

Gray eyed the drink, and his taste buds shriveled. "I
wouldn't put that in my stomach."

Sunny hiccuped again. She knocked back a bit of the
potion, then propped her chin in her hand, cocking an
accusing eyebrow Doc's way. "You must have done
somethin' or Ms. Rose wouldn't have taken off. Spit it
out."

Doc snorted. "Goldurn it. All I said was Eulah Fish-
bine makes mighty good fried chicken."

Gray shut his eyes against the words. "Don't you
know to never, ever compliment another woman's

cooking? Especially when the other woman just got married and Ms. Rose wants to get married more than anything."

Doc's jaw went slack and his eyes widened. He dropped his half-eaten sandwich back on the plate. "Married? To who, for crying out loud?"

Sunny let out a loud belch. "You. Even I know that and I know nothing. I have amnesia."

"Ms. Rose wants to marry me? Poppycock. She and Johnny, rest his soul, were married thirty-five years. Johnny was my dearest friend. I was best man at his wedding. I can't go courting Johnny's wife."

Gray gave Doc a hard look. "Johnny's been dead seven years, and if you don't do something quick, Junior Jones is going to snap her right up. Heard he's been sending her sappy poems and big chocolate hearts and pricing diamond rings over in Silver Grove."

Doc's face reddened and a vein popped out on his forehead. "J-junior? That bald-headed pipsqueak. Bet he's after Rose's money. Johnny's got to be flipping in his grave."

Sunny swayed. "Flipping or not, you better do somethin' quick."

Her eyes rolled around like BBs in a box. She slipped from her stool, and Gray caught her under the arms before she hit the floor.

She tipped her head back and frowned up at him. "What are you doing here, Gray McBride? You're supposed to be out with Margie. You guys get married yet?"

Gray hauled her back onto the stool and she sagged like a sack of potatoes...very nice potatoes. "I sure hope you found that drink you were wanting, Sunny Kelly, because you're going to pay one hell of a price for it in the morning."

"I don't hafta pay, Gray. I own the bar." She gave him a cockeyed grin.

"You need to sleep it off." He didn't want to carry her upstairs. Holding her in his arms would kill what control he had. But how could he ask someone else to carry her without explaining why he wouldn't?

Did staying uninvolved with a woman have to be so damn complicated? Usually he just walked away and it was over with. Why not this time?

She burped and draped her arms around his neck. Smitty said, "You take care of the boss and we'll clean things up down here."

Gray plastered a grin onto his face. "Hey, I can clean up."

Sunny's eyes closed and her head dropped onto his shoulder. *Great.* He picked her up, one arm under her knees, the other supporting her back. She felt warm and soft, as though she belonged here. He started for the inside stairway that led to her apartment. How was he supposed to keep his mind off Sunny's sweet little body snuggled close to his? He needed to get her up there quick, put her to bed and then run.

She stared at him bleary-eyed. "Where are we goin', cowboy?"

He reached the top landing, fumbled with opening

the door and went into the room where he'd changed his clothes. "*You're* going to bed."

Her head dropped back, exposing her lovely throat. She grinned. "Wanna join me?"

He nearly dropped her on top of Six but managed to set her on the bed instead. He unwound her arms from his neck and steadied her. "You smell like a distillery."

"You smell wonderful. And you're all tall and strong and gorgeous." She opened one eye and peeked at Six. "Isn't he gorgeous?"

"You're drunk."

"Na."

He yanked open a drawer and found a huge blue T-shirt, obviously Bessy's. "Here," he said. "You can sleep in—" When he glanced back, she was flat on her back, arms spread, eyes shut, breathing slow. "Sunny?"

"Subchapter S corporation, triple tax-exempt bond, rent stabilization."

"You need to cancel your subscription to *Reader's Digest*. You're obsessed with it."

He pulled off his hat and ran his hand through his hair as he continued to gaze at her. "And I'm obsessed with you."

"Accelerated cost-recovery system, net operating loss, repurchase agreement."

He cranked up the window air conditioner, went to the bathroom and ran a towel under the faucet, found aspirin in the medicine cabinet and got a glass of water. He put the towel on Sunny's forehead, the rest on the nightstand, and covered her with an afghan from the foot of the old iron bed. "You're going to be all right, Sunny Kelly."

He studied her smooth skin and slightly parted lips. The front of his jeans felt two sizes too small. "I just wish to hell I was."

He took the wet cloth from Sunny's forehead and slapped it on his own face. *Get a grip.* He headed back down to the bar. Doc had left; Norm and Art said goodnight and made for the door. Jean and Smitty wandered off to their apartment. He envied the young couple…basement apartment and all. They were truly in love, cared for each other and had a baby on the way. Tomorrow he'd stop at one of those shops on Main Street and get a crib and some other stuff sent over. Least he could do, since he was the one who'd introduced them. He was getting pretty good at this matchmaking stuff. First Smitty and Jean, now Joe and Maggie.

Gray locked the place up, turned off the lights, cracked a long neck and parked himself on a stool. The smell of Windex and varnish overpowered stale smoke and old beer. His reflection in the mirror stared back at him.

When he'd decided to be mayor, Sunny Kelly hadn't existed…at least to him. But she sure as hell did now and he was more than a little crazy about her. And not just her golden hair and sassy smile and fine shape, but the way she took in "strays" and made them feel welcome and important. She had spunk and determination and made everything more fun than it should be.

Trouble was, if he got involved with Sunny Kelly, her connections with a rowdy cowboy saloon and her being a Reno showgirl wouldn't convince the good citizens of Tranquility one iota that he'd changed his ways. Under normal circumstances he didn't give a flying fig what the town thought, but if he wanted to be mayor he had to care. *Damn, he hated politics.* Why would anyone get into this of his own free will?

Gray polished off the beer and stood. Going home held little appeal. He'd be farther from Sunny and right now that wasn't what he wanted at all. Hell, he wanted her close, cuddled up next to him, both of them upstairs in her bed.

The room suddenly felt stifling. He opened a window, then pulled the sheet from the pool table and dropped it on a chair. A cue stick bisected the green felt and he pulled three balls from the leather side pockets. He'd shoot a little pool, do some thinking, get rid of some frustration. Too bad he couldn't do a few rounds on Widow Maker. But Leroy would hear that and come running…snoopy little man that he was. With the front porch gone, Leroy couldn't watch him play pool.

Moonlight through the window let him see well enough to sink the three-ball, then the five and the eight. Still he had no answers and his frustration hadn't subsided one inch. He lay across the table, keeping his boots off the felt, resting his head on the bumper. He stared at the beamed ceiling. He thought of Sunny asleep upstairs and how he wanted her and how all the

pool and thinking in the world wouldn't get them together. What a complete mess.

SUNNY CRAWLED from the shower, wrapped a towel
around her wet hair, pulled on one of Bessy's robes that
resembled a tablecloth with a hole in the middle, then
padded through the dark bedroom. The digital clock
flashed 4:00 a.m. At least she felt better than she had
at 11:00 p.m. Thanks be to aspirin and a hot shower.

She couldn't do bright lights yet… Heck, she could
barely walk…so the room stayed dark except for the
full moon hanging outside her window. Her mouth
tasted like cotton balls dipped in gasoline. A Coke
would help, and maybe some Oreos.

Why Coke and Oreos? Another little mystery in the
unknown life of Sunny Kelly. Maybe if she ate a cookie
her memory would return. It was worth a try. Nothing
else had worked.

She headed downstairs, turned the corner and spied
a body flopped across the pool table. One of those
drunks Smitty had warned her about. She grabbed a
mop hanging beside the fire extinguisher. Protection in
case this was a mean drunk. She rolled her eyes at her
ferocious watchdog snoozing blissfully in the corner
and headed for the body. She banged the mop handle
across the end of the table to wake her guest and a stab-
bing headache shot through her brain like a bullet. *Not
a swift move on her part. Ouch!* "Does this look like
the Holiday Inn? Sleep it off somewhere else, buster."

The guy sat up, dangling his legs over the table.

"What the hell are you doing, Kelly? Trying to scare me half to death? You're going to ruin your pool table."

"Gray? Why are you here?"

He ran his hand through his hair as if trying to get awake. Faint light silhouetted his broad shoulders and trim build. Why couldn't he be fat and bald? Heck, even that wouldn't help. He'd turned his life upside down to help his family, and you didn't meet that kind of guy every day. She'd fall for him no matter what…and she was indeed falling for him. She didn't want to. What was the point when they had no future together?

"Needed to do some thinking."

"While lying on a pool table?"

He rolled his broad shoulders as if trying to get out the kinks. "It was that or the bar, and I thought I might fall off it and break my neck. Pool table has sides." He let out a deep sigh and scrutinized her for a moment. "Why were you drinking tonight?"

"Why?" Her gaze met his and the mop slid from her hand, landing onto the wooden floor with a whap. Oh, boy. What was she going to tell him? She'd gotten sloshed because she didn't want to think about him and nothing else worked? Then again, getting sloshed hadn't helped, either. "A house drink is an interesting marketing concept." She shrugged. "Though what I came up with was closer to battery acid and nowhere near interesting…unless you're a car mechanic."

She touched his cheek, feeling his scratchy beard, watching his pulse beat in his neck, knowing she should keep her hands to herself. But he was so strong, so dependable, so handsome… "Sorry things didn't work out with you and Maggie."

He didn't say a word but took her hand from his face, held it for moment, then planted a warm kiss in her palm, sending shivers up her arm. He pulled her close and nestled her between his thighs. The heat of his body surrounded her and she swallowed hard.

"Maggie and I weren't meant to be. I don't know any show tunes."

She should run upstairs and lock the door before she got any more involved with Gray…and she felt more involved by the second. He kissed her other palm.

She really should run. But her feet wouldn't move. And he still held her hand. How could she run when he had her hand? "Did you carry me upstairs last night?"

Night sounds drifted through the window; the world felt still and peaceful…except for the thudding of her heart. "Did…did I come on to you?"

His eyes turned the color of the midnight sky. "Do you want to now?" He kissed the inside curve of her elbow and she nearly melted.

"What about the election?"

"It's four o'clock in the morning. Nester's off sawing logs somewhere. Screw the election. Right now it's just us."

Us. She nibbled at her bottom lip. "I wasn't really trying to find a drink for the bar tonight. I was trying to forget about you and Maggie. I was at the Mill

Pond...for a while...with Elizabeth. Then I left—I couldn't take seeing you with Maggie and not...me."

His eyes widened in disbelief. "You're kidding. You're the one who set this date up."

She let out a deep breath. "Trust me, I would not kid about something that ended with me drinking Tabasco sauce and Coke with a pickle chaser to try to get you and Maggie out of my brain." She played with a lock of his rich dark hair. "The date didn't turn out the way I'd planned, and I don't just mean with the piano player."

He unwound the towel from her hair and dropped it on the floor. He looked into her eyes, gently wove his fingers through her damp curls, massaging her scalp, then her nape. He kissed her nose, her chin, then her lips, making her insides warm and heavy with wanting him.

He ran his hands down her arms to her waist and nuzzled her neck. "Things haven't been easy since you got here."

"I think they're getting better." Her gaze found his.

"We should go upstairs."

"Too far. And somewhere between here and there we could come to our senses and realize this is not a great idea. I don't want to come to my senses right now, Gray. Maybe tomorrow."

His eyes widened a fraction. "You sure you want to do this?"

"I'm not the one sinking my own campaign."

He tipped her chin. "I hate sneaking around. But I

can't back out of the election now. Dillon will never give me any real responsibility around the ranch if I don't finish this and win."

"You have to take care of your family." She kissed his cheek and whispered in his ear, "It's one of the things I like about you. And that you have a nice butt."

"So I've heard."

"Smitty has a big mouth." She felt him chuckle and kissed him, her lips savoring the feel of his, his arms surrounding her, pulling her tight to his chest. All man, all rugged cowboy. He smelled of pine trees, rich earth, Texas sunshine, and she burned for him.

He stood, their bodies hip to hip, his erection pressing into her belly. She wasn't the only one burning. He scooped her up in his arms and sat her gently on the table. This time he nestled himself between her legs.

She said, "Whenever I look at this pool table I'll think of tonight."

He kissed her. "And have some damn good memories." He kissed her again, his tongue mating with hers. His hands slid under her flowing robe, cupping the sides of her breasts, his thumb grazing her left nipple, then her right, and she gasped in sheer pleasure.

"It's not exactly where I thought we'd make love."

"You thought about this?" Her mouth was so dry she could barely get the words out.

"You have no idea what you do to me."

Her blood flowed fast, like the Dow-Jones Industrial Average on a multimillion-share day. *Where the heck had that come from?*

"You're incredibly beautiful, you're a one-woman rescue squad and I admire you. I'm saying all this while you still have your clothes on so you know these words aren't entirely fueled by lust."

She laughed. "Maybe a little lust?"

His eyes narrowed; a wicked smile played at his lips. "Babe, when I'm with you there's always lust." He kissed a soft spot behind her ear. His hands cupped her breasts, his hands sure and gentle. "About these clothes…"

"About protection…"

"Always protection." And in one swift move, he flipped off her robe and dropped it onto the floor.

GRAY'S INSIDES clenched. He actually felt light-headed. She was incredible. Her skin shone in the moonlight; her lovely bare thighs circling his waist were erotic as hell, her breasts full and firm…waiting for his touch…and more. "You're gorgeous." His breath came quick, his mouth as parched as the south pasture in August. "You're perfect." He could barely speak, but he wanted her to know.

She kissed him, her lips parted, her tongue tasting, teasing, driving him wild. He fondled her back, so smooth from her nape to her derriere. She shivered in his arms. "Cold?"

Her eyes widened a fraction. "It's like a blast furnace in here and one of us still has his clothes on and the other can't wait forever."

She undid the top button of his shirt, then the next. She tugged the material from his pants, finished unbuttoning, then reached for his belt. His gaze held hers as she unbuckled…then unzipped, the sound echoing through the room. His erection strained against his briefs and he thought he'd lose his mind as her hand stroked his arousal, her heat through the thin barrier fueling his.

He didn't want the barrier.

He pulled off his boots, then his pants and briefs. He took the condom from his wallet and made himself ready for her. Her eyes widened and her mouth fell open. He asked, "Are you okay?"

"I…I don't know if I've ever done this before, and you're so…big. How could I forget something so big."

"You're a…a virgin? Or are you just trying to build my ego?"

"I don't know if I'm a virgin. I doubt it. I'm a Reno showgirl and somewhere in my late twenties. Virginity doesn't seem like much of a possibility."

"Maybe we shouldn't…"

She grabbed him by the shoulders and gritted her teeth, looking him dead in the eye. "Now's not the time for *shouldn't*."

He snagged the sheet from the chair, spread it on the table, then hitched himself up beside her and slowly leaned her back. He studied her, memorized her beauty as he traced his finger over her breasts and down her middle to her navel. She quivered under his touch, her eyes darkening, her reactions making him hotter than ever. "We'll take it slow." Though he had no idea how to do that.

"Gray." She swallowed as she ran her hands over his chest, tangling her fingers in his hair. "Forget slow."

"I don't think you're a virgin." His control plunged; his desire escalated. He positioned himself over her, relishing the feel of her hardening nipples against his chest, the soft curls nestling his erection, her legs and arms wrapping around his back. "You are so lovely, an incredible lover."

Using what little control that remained, he eased himself into her. She was hot and wet and open for him, welcoming him into her sweet body. His blood surged and he kissed her damp lips. Her fingers dug into his shoulders; every fiber of his body went hard with wanting.

"Oh, Gray," she gasped, her back arching. Her legs tightened, taking him deeper still, destroying the last shreds of restraint, and he filled her again and again till they climaxed together, their bodies and worlds uniting.

He didn't want this to end. Making love to Sunny was amazing. He'd never felt so alive, so complete. Then he thought of the election. *Well, damn.*

She stirred under him and whispered, "Gray. The sheriff's snooping around again."

"Honey, I've heard a man's equipment called a lot of things, but—"

"*Not that.* The real sheriff. Don't you see the flashlight on the walls? I don't think he got a good look, since the porch is gone."

"Light? Hell, I thought it was the aftereffects of incredible sex."

"Men!" She gave one big shove and he landed on his back in the middle of the pool table, spread-eagled as Sunny flipped the sheet over him. "This is not the perfect ending to perfect sex."

"Sunny?" Sheriff Leroy's voice sounded from outside. "Everything all right in there?" He rapped his flashlight against the wooden side.

She whispered to Gray, "Don't move a muscle."

She found her robe and pulled it on while hurrying to the door. She yanked it open. "Sheriff," she said, a huge smile plastered on her face. "How nice to see you so early in the morning."

He moseyed in, casting his light to corners, floor and ceiling. "Thought I heard something from outside while making my rounds. Wanted to make sure you were okay and no one had broken in. After Bessy passed, Smitty and Jean had problems with freeloaders helping themselves to the booze, so I keep an eye on the place."

"Nobody here but me and Six. We were talking about…the day." Leroy gave her a curious look as she stationed herself between him and the pool table. "Just getting an early start…like you. I'm down for a Coke and to check the place out."

He pushed his hat back on his head. "The Smokehouse sure is shaping up. Mind turning on the light and letting me see the place?"

"Ah, the fuse box…it's been acting up. Not enough power for the new things we're putting in. We disconnected the lights…for now." She smiled slowly, corralling him back toward the door. "Sure appreciate you stopping by."

"My pleasure." He tipped his hat. "Isn't that Gray's truck out front?"

Crimany. "Broke. It's broken. So he had one of the hands stop by and get him."

"After his date over at the Mill Pond?"

"Yep, that's it. Just like you said. The thing went kaput right in front of The Smokehouse." She tried to crowd him out the door, but he stood firm.

"Not like Gray to just let his truck sit here overnight. Maybe he left the key under the mat. Maybe I should see if I can fix it for him, since he's tied up with the rodeo and all. Always been pretty good with engines, kind of a hobby of mine."

"I bet the Hungry Heifer's serving up breakfast. Hotcakes, warm maple syrup, sausage." Her stomach growled at the menu. "Besides, Gray will probably come first thing this morning for the truck—I'm sure of it."

"Heard he stopped by here last night, too."

The gossip mill was alive and well in Tranquility, Texas. "To…call the Lazy K and get a ride home."

Leroy ambled over to the bar, way too close to the pool table…*and Gray's clothes scattered on the floor.*

"Eggs over easy, fresh-squeezed juice, whole-wheat toast. Bet the Heifer's serving right now."

"I hate whole-wheat toast." He eyed the pool table. "I always loved this table. Played many a game here."

He took two steps toward the table and the clothes.

Sunny's heart almost stopped. "Hot biscuits, honey, strawberry jam." *Please let that be drool collecting at the corner of Leroy's mouth.*

He paused and stroked his chin. "I could do with a bit of breakfast before I fix the truck."

"Absolutely. Breakfast is the most important meal of the day."

"All right."

He started to turn, then didn't. He stared at the table and Sunny saw her life pass before her eyes...what little she could remember of it. "You shouldn't be storing stuff on your pool table. Gets it out of balance."

"I'll remember that."

He tipped his hat again. "I'll be back later with my toolbox and you can give me a tour of what you've done to the place."

The sheriff exited, and Sunny stood in the doorway smiling and waving till he was down the next block and turned for the Hungry Heifer.

"That was close." At the sound of Gray's voice, she spun around in time to see him standing buck naked in the first rays of dawn. Then he ruined the show by putting on his pants.

She didn't know what was worse—Leroy driving her nuts with his nosiness and poking around all the time, or Gray driving her nuts with his great body. "You better get out of here now before anyone else sees you."

He snatched his boots in one hand and shirt in the other and came to the door. He kissed her hard, then winked. "One for the road."

He got in the truck, cranked over the engine and rode off into the sunrise. How in the world did she ever get involved with Gray McBride? And how in the world was she going to get *uninvolved*? She glanced at the pool table. This wasn't a good way to get uninvolved.

No matter how great the lovemaking…and it was great…she and Gray could not go on like this. She leaned against the doorjamb. The two of them together, making love, was hard on her heart…in more ways than one. Somehow she had to stay away from him, and that wouldn't be easy, since they had a rodeo to plan.

Chapter Five

After Sunny helped Smitty, Norm and Art hammer the front steps into place, they all stood back and admired the new porch as Jean served glasses of lemonade. Sunny held her glass high for a toast and the others followed. "To The Smokehouse, bigger and better than ever."

They clinked glasses and gulped under the sweltering afternoon sun. Smitty rested his hand on her shoulder. "Well, the outside's done and we're making progress on the inside. The question is, oh guru of the finances, are we running out of money?"

Sunny massaged her forehead. "To date, our cash flow is still liquid. If remuneration becomes an issue we'll consider deficit financing, and—"

Smitty rolled his eyes. "English, please."

"Why do I do that? The words just kind of pop out. I must have been reading more than *Reader's Digest*."

"Yeah," Norm agreed. "The dictionary."

Sunny chuckled. "What it means is, we have money as long as we don't have to pay for everything at once.

There's enough in Bessy's account for the next mortgage payment, which is due tomorrow. Paying for supplies and rodeo advertising will have to wait till we open. Since the rodeo's only six days away, and the crowds will be in town for our opening the night before and we should make a killing, we shouldn't have a problem. We'll donate a portion of those profits to the town. It will improve the saloon's image with the citizens and attract customers, especially the women. Women here are very civic-minded. Seems they're the ones who keep Tranquility hopping."

Norm laughed. "Now, *that* I understand."

Sunny grinned. "Me, too. I've got to see Gray about setting up for the rodeo and give him flyers to pass out to the cowboys so they can sign up for the events. There are posters in the back room. Can you all start putting them up around town today? The sooner the better."

Jean's eyes sparkled. "This is so exciting."

Sunny nodded at Jean's rounded middle under a yellow print skirt. "*That's* what's exciting. Two more months?"

Jean blushed. "And…and Smitty's asked me to marry him…before the baby comes…so he, or she, will have a proper daddy and all."

Norm and Art let out an ear-piercing yelp and Sunny felt tears sting her eyes. She hugged Jean, then Smitty, as Art and Norm thumped him on the back.

Sunny nodded at the saloon. "You should have the reception here as part of the reopening. The Smokehouse is going to be more of a gals-and-guys place, not just a cowboy bar. Everything'll be fresh and clean, and we'll have flowers and music and cake, and everyone can come and you'll get presents. We'll have a wonderful party. We'll supply the beer for the first hour, and after that everyone's on their own. It'll be fun and—"

Jean burst into tears and everyone froze. Smitty looked as if a horse had tromped on his foot. Art and Norm weren't breathing. Sunny put her arms around Jean. "Or not. What was I thinking? We don't have to do this. It was a bad idea. A stupid suggestion by a woman who has amnesia and—"

"No, no." Jean choked back sobs and grabbed Sunny's hand in a tight squeeze. "It's just that you all are so kind." She glanced from Norm to Art. She gazed lovingly at Smitty. "My mama kicked me out when I got pregnant, said I was nothing but trouble, and I believed her. I never thought I'd find a man like Smitty and now friends like you. And a wedding and reception?" Her voice cracked and more tears flowed. Smitty gathered her in his arms and the tender expression on his face made Sunny cry. Norm and Art weren't far behind.

Sunny grinned and swiped tears. "Then it's settled. July third you're getting married and we're throwing one wingding of a do here at The Smokehouse. This is just the way Auntie would have wanted it. She would have loved it." She winked at Jean. "We'll get you a lovely dress and—"

"Wait." Smitty sobered. "I hate to be a party pooper, but I can't pay for—"

"Of course you can." Sunny beamed. "Because the cost is the use of your Nova. If I don't get to the Lazy K today, there won't be a rodeo or a grand opening that's going to save all of our backsides."

Smitty fished the keys from his pocket and handed them to Sunny, along with a big smile. "What a deal."

She headed upstairs, having no idea how she'd pay for all the things she'd just promised. She'd float the bills till after the opening and then pay everybody off with the profits…there had to be profits. Nothing like walking a financial tightrope with no safety net to catch her if she fell.

She grabbed a quick shower, then went downstairs and picked up the remaining flyers and posters for the rodeo. The rest of The Smokehouse gang was probably already hanging ads and passing out information. A big brown bag lay on the bar. Cement. With a knife sticking out? Why would someone kill a bag of cement on her bar? A note stuck through by the blade said, *Pay up or else.*

"Whoa." Sunny pulled out the knife, wrapped it in a towel and threw it and the note away. What if Jean saw this? Not the thing for a pregnant lady to witness. It would scare her to death…just as it did Sunny.

Why *Pay up or else*? She owed money to the bank for the mortgage, but not till tomorrow. *Some reminder.* And why cement? Maybe the hardware store had sent it over. She owed that bill, too. The stores in Tranquility sure played hardball. Didn't these people ever hear of a phone call? A note...something friendly? Wasn't that how things were done in a small town? Apparently not *this* small town. She'd better take care of the bill before they left any more messages.

She dropped off a check to the bank and the hardware store. Everyone was paid...for now, and as she took the road out of town to the Lazy K she decided she had nothing to worry about.

The Nova felt more like an oven on four wheels than a car, and by the time she killed the engine in front of the main house she was hot and sticky. Horses grazed in the side pasture and a breeze gently swung the hanging baskets of geraniums on the porch. Animals dotted the landscape, but there was no one around. "Gray?"

"Hey, Reno. Over here."

Her gaze followed Gray's voice, and she spotted him in the back corral. She waved and took the gravel lane, her boots crunching on the stones that wound a path between flower gardens, vegetable gardens, a sandbox and swing set. Gray wasn't alone in the corral. The twins were there, along with a wooden barrel perched on four legs, complete with a smiling cow's head and rope tail. "Working on a new breed of cattle?"

"Teaching the boys how to rope," he called. "You know you could run. I'm not getting any younger waiting for you."

The twins made whooping sounds and jumped around Gray in little circles. As she climbed through the white rungs of the fence she realized Gray wasn't exactly standing in the middle of the ring because he wanted to. He was tied there. To a post. And the boys' jumping resembled more of a victory dance. "What happened to you?"

The boys sang, *"We got Uncle Gray. We got Uncle Gray."*

"You look completely helpless."

"That's because I *am* completely helpless. I was showing the boys how to lasso and—"

She chuckled and he growled. "We were practicing with the lasso, throwing the rope over my hands. I was standing by the post…and before I knew what happened they threw a rope over me *and the post* and pulled, and I tripped and—"

Her chuckle escalated into laughter and the kids sang louder. "Do cowboys get tied up with their own rope often?"

"I'm so glad I supplied you with some entertainment for the day, but will you just untie me? The rope's twisted around my back and I can't get to it with my hands wound together."

"A Kodak moment?"

"Untie me, dammit."

"Uncle Gray said a bad word. Uncle Gray said a bad word. Mommy's going to wash his mouth out. Mommy's going to wash his mouth out."

She'd come out here expecting to see a rough-and-tumble sexy cowboy. She'd found Uncle Gray, hassled babysitter. She swallowed hard, suddenly feeling more attracted to Gray McBride, family man and terrific uncle, than to Gray McBride, cowboy. And that was going some. He had a family, a wonderful family, who loved him and he truly loved them. How could anyone ask for more than that?

"Where's Dillon and everybody else?"

"Mom's visiting friends in Amarillo till after the Fourth, and it's Cook's day off. A few of the hands are on vacation and the rest are checking on herds in the south pasture. Elizabeth has a doctor's appointment and Dillon is busy with ranch business that he insisted only *he* could do. Not that I mind watching the boys, but I can help with the ranch if their daddy would just get that through his thick skull."

"Daddy has a thick skull, Daddy has a thick skull."

"Great."

Gray really did need to win that election for his own sake and for Dillon's. The twins would be half-grown before he knew it. Sunny said to the boys, "Gee, it's hot out here. Let's untie Uncle Gray and get some lemonade and cookies. We can put peanut butter on them and make cookie sandwiches. What do you say?"

They stopped their victory dance and grinned up at her, the personification of innocence. "Yay!" they yelled, and helped her unwind the rope from around Gray. She loosened his hands, remembering how wonderful his hands were. Strong yet gentle, gliding over her bare skin, turning her insides to jelly and doing the very same thing now with her just thinking about last night. *Good grief.*

The last tangle loosened and the boys cheered. "We want lemonade." They ran off for the house in a dead run, then made a detour and aimed for their swing set.

She wagged her head in amazement. "If I could bottle that kind of energy and sell it, The Smokehouse would be on easy street forever."

He took her hand. "You look gorgeous today."

"Is this flattery for keeping my mouth shut about the kids tying you up?"

He feigned a wounded expression. "Would I do such thing?"

"In a heartbeat. But your secret's safe with me. I won't tell Nester. He'd probably figure out some way to use it against you."

Gray heaved a deep sigh. "He doesn't need it. He's already come up with something better. His new campaign slogan is, 'More taxes for the rich and less for everyone else.' He's playing to the fact that the McBrides have money and he doesn't and he's one of the good old boys and not a spoiled rich boy like me. Never mind that we work like hell at the Lazy K and the McBrides financed the new wing at the library, an auditorium for the high school and fifty acres for a park, and we give kids jobs during the summer."

"And if you bring any of those things up it'll appear as if you're buying your way to be mayor and play right into his hands."

"Bingo. And it's one of the reasons we can't just donate a portion of a new firehouse." They watched the kids swing for a few moments. "I need to get back on track with my own campaign, or I won't have a chance of winning. I need to come up with something."

This did not make her feel warm and fuzzy. "Meaning?"

He ran his hand through his hair. "The Smokehouse is still my best—"

"No way." She glared at him, hands on hips to add sternness to her words. "You just keep away from my saloon. You're doing the rodeo, remember? It will be great and you'll be the town hero and the revenue from the rodeo will go toward building a brand-new firehouse somewhere else."

He held out his hands, palms up. "We won't make that much money off the rodeo."

"How do you know? Wait and see. It's going to be big. Huge."

"Tranquility doesn't have enough people to make anything big and huge, and time's running out. I have to do something now."

"Get a new campaign going of your own."

"I'll look weak if I abandon the one I have. Besides, it's a good one, something that benefits the whole town."

"You are not getting my saloon, Gray McBride. It's not just for me but for Art and Norm and Six and Jean and Smitty. In fact, Smitty and Jean are having their wedding reception there on the third along with our grand opening."

"Hell. When did this happen?"

"Today." She poked him in the chest. "Forget the saloon."

"The town needs a bigger fire department, I need to win the election and The Smokehouse is smack in the middle. I can't forget that."

"How can you do this to me?"

"How can *you* do this to *me*?"

She went to the Nova, where she yanked open the door, jutted her chin and pointed to the corral. "I should have let the sun cook your ungrateful carcass and turn it into buzzard bait."

She got in and fired the engine. To think she'd made love with Gray last night. And she'd enjoyed it. A lot. Well, it wouldn't happen again, that she was sure of. The jerk wanted to take her saloon.

SUNNY CLOSED the business ledger on the desk, then gazed out the apartment window with Six. She wanted to forget about finances and a certain cowboy who should be hung by his toenails till he turned blue; Six waited for a certain poodle due to come prancing down the sidewalk any moment now.

Sunny gave the rocker a push and listened to the old floorboards creak as if chanting, *Gray's a jerk, Gray's a jerk, Gray's a jerk.* They watched the Nova head down Oak Street. Smitty and Jean heading out of town for some fun somewhere…at least, she hoped so. They'd both worked so hard on fixing the saloon.

Doc and Norm walked into the Durango Diner for supper; Doc's glasses still held together by a Band-Aid, his hair a bit shabby, his clothes mussed. "If Ms. Rose doesn't get come home soon Doc's going to look like a bum."

Six barked and licked her face.

"Yuck. Have you been sneaking over to the Chili House for handouts again? Next time beg a mint." She patted Six. "Well, what have we here? I do believe that's Lucky Tanner and the lovely Mimi also going into the Durango Diner. Smitty says Tanner is one of the biggest men in town and knows how to change a carburetor in his sleep. What is he doing with a prissy poodle done out in pink ribbons for a pet?"

Six barked and wagged his tail, a devilish twinkle in his eye. "Thoughts like that can get you in trouble, you know."

Art followed Lucky, then two more cowboys. "Business is booming at the diner. Must be barbecue night. Smells wonderful." Her stomach growled. "Sure could do with some Durango barbecue. We could get one order and split it. "'Course, we can't sit too close to Mimi, since Tanner's still a little miffed about me being involved and blowing his gas station to kingdom come."

Sunny glanced down at the ledger. "You should know, if the rodeo next week doesn't bring in business, we—as in you and me—will be eating cat food instead of barbecue for a really long time."

Six whined.

"Don't panic just yet. We should be okay."

Six jumped down, ran in circles and barked.

"See, you're panicking already, and that's not good. You'll get an ulcer. The saloon's almost finished and people are starting to talk the place up. Word of mouth is the best advertisement."

Six barked again. He pawed the floor.

"Okay, okay. We'll go eat. Keep your fur on." She glanced back outside. The sun had dropped a bit deeper into the western sky, the birds darted here and there looking for dinner, little puffs of smoke curled outside the window.

Smoke? She stood and went to the window. Six tugged at her pant leg, nearly toppling her off balance. Something was burning and it wasn't barbecue. Six whined and dragged her toward the door for all he was worth, making her hop on one foot. "What are you doing, you nutty dog? I want to see what's going on."

The curls outside thickened, rising from somewhere below. *The saloon was below!*

"Fire?" Her eyes nearly popped from her head. She faced Six. *"The saloon's on fire! Ohmygod."*

She touched the doorknob. It was cool, so she yanked the door open and ran down the inside stairway behind Six, rounded the corner—and stopped dead. Flames lapped at the walls in the front corner by the ladders and paint cans. They danced across her newly varnished floors, spreading, threatening Widow Maker.

No! She couldn't let this happen to her bar, her bull. This was Texas. People protected what was theirs…especially their cattle. She dashed to the front door and shoved Six outside, then snatched the phone and dialed

O because the numbers she was supposed to dial refused to compute. She yelled, "FireatTheSmokehouse!"

Grabbing the extinguisher next to the mop, she gritted her teeth, then charged into the flames. She pulled the pin, aimed the hose and... *Nothing?* She shook the canister. No squirting, no white foamy stuff, zip.

The flames spread, getting taller and eating up more floor. She soaked two bar towels in the sink and attacked the growing flames again, whacking them back. *Take that, and that.*

Sirens blared. Her eyes stung; tears streamed down her face. From the smoke, she told herself. Truth be told, she was scared to death.

She whammed the flames again, not making much headway but keeping them away from her bull. Was she a good Texan or what? The sirens stopped in front of the bar. Gee, that was fast...maybe because The Smokehouse was right in front of the firehouse. An unexpected perk.

Four firefighters in full gear barged through the front door, carrying hoses and axes. Axes? Oh, no, not axes. "This is a no-ax bar."

One of the firefighters yelled to Sunny, "Get the hell out of here." He aimed his hose at the flames and let loose with a cannon of water.

She swung at more flames. "My bar, my bull."

Someone snatched her from behind. "Hey!" She couldn't turn to see who it was as she stumbled backward out the door, onto the front porch, down the steps, past the fire truck with lights strobing, Six barking and the gathering crowd.

"Let me go." She spun around and faced Gray.

"You?"

"Don't you have enough sense to get out of a burning building when told to? What the hell were you doing in there?"

Norm put a big arm around her shoulder. "Are you okay? I saw the flames from the diner."

"I'm fine," she said to Norm. Then to Gray, "And for your information, what I was doing in there was saving my saloon. 'Course, I don't expect you to understand that, since you'd like nothing better than to shut the place down."

She glanced back at the smoke and smoldering debris and felt her heart sink to her toes. How could this happen? They were so close. Her eyes narrowed. Maybe too close. "The question is, Gray McBride, why are *you* here?"

She wiped sweat and grime from her face as a mixture of adrenaline, fear and helplessness shot though her veins at rocket speed. She growled, "But that's a really dumb question, since I already know why you're here. *You torched my saloon.*"

There was a collected gasp from the crowd, who had suddenly found her and Gray's conversation a lot more interesting than the petered-out fire.

"I *what?*" His eyes rounded.

Smitty shook his head. "You don't mean it, Sunny. You're upset. Gray wouldn't do something like that."

She pushed her hair from her face and swiped her runny nose with the back of her hand. "He wants to close the saloon down and make it part of the new firehouse. Everybody knows that. In fact, when I went out to the Lazy K this afternoon he made that clear as glass."

Gray pushed his hat to the back of his head. His eyes hardened. "You're calling me an arsonist?"

Norm sucked in air through clenched teeth. "Oh, boy."

The crowd went dead quiet, looking from Gray to Sunny and back again. Smitty, Jean, Norm and Art backed up. Six hid under the porch. The fire in the bar was out, but smoke curled from the door. One window was broken and black was everywhere. It matched her mood perfectly.

He glared. "You really think I'd set fire to the bar? That I'd risk burning down this whole town and people getting hurt to have my way?"

"No one else has a motive, cowboy. All my plans have just gone up in smoke, while yours have just taken a giant leap forward. That makes you a number-one suspect in my book. And if you're so innocent, why are you here and not at the Lazy K, minding cows? Answer me that one."

His lips thinned into a straight line. The crowd took a step back as if fearful something might explode. Sunny took a step forward, the toes of her gym shoes touching the tips of his worn boots.

"For your information, the reason I was in town was to drop off fence for the rodeo next week."

One of the firefighters approached. "Well, *someone* sure torched the place. We found a burn line from outside to a pile of rags in the corner. Only one part of the bar suffered damage."

"See," Sunny said to Gray. "It didn't just start by itself."

The firefighter undid his big coat and continued, "Nothing structural, just cosmetic. The apartment upstairs is okay, but the apartment in the basement is a mess. Everything there is pretty much ruined due to water damage. Probably some kids with nothing better to do than play with matches started this. We'll ask around. At least no one was hurt."

Sunny felt ill and it had nothing to do with the smoke. "Heck of a wedding present."

Gray said, "Smitty and Jean can stay at the Lazy K." He adjusted his hat on his head, turned and crossed the street just as Elizabeth's white minivan swung around the corner and stopped beside him. They talked for a moment, then Elizabeth parked, got out and headed Sunny's way.

Norm put his hand on her shoulder. "Art and I will go check on the damage. Try not to piss anyone else off till we get back, okay? It's bad for business."

"But Gray burned down the bar."

Norm rolled his big shoulders in a way that suggested he didn't quite agree.

When Elizabeth reached Sunny she hugged her tight. She needed a hug right now. Fighting fires did not come easy to a Reno showgirl…at least not this one. Elizabeth stepped back and took Sunny's hand. "Is anyone hurt? What in the world happened here? Are you okay?"

"Scared, rattled, angry. Pick one…or all. And my brain is Swiss cheese. Not a good mix with amnesia. And to top it all off—you'll love this—I accused Gray of setting fire to The Smokehouse. I've clearly lost my mind."

"You what?" Elizabeth looked as if she'd been struck by lightning—which was exactly how Sunny felt.

Sunny held her hands up in surrender. "I know, I know. It was stupid and dumb and I said it because I was terrified and all my plans just bit the dust and Gray is the one who will benefit most by this." She rolled her eyes. "Ten minutes ago that all seemed very logical."

"You really think he'd burn down the bar?"

"In his dreams he probably burned the place to the ground. But in reality, no." She let out a deep breath. "So now my saloon and his election are both in the toilet."

"But you still have the bar."

"Sort of." She hitched her chin toward the smoldering building. "It's a mess and I'm broke and there's not money enough to…" Her eyes connected with Elizabeth's and the Swiss cheese feeling vanished, replaced by a thread of common sense. "Holy moly. Insurance. Your father wouldn't have the mortgage on this place without insurance, would he?"

"Amazing how you know such things."

"I'm telling you, *Reader's Digest* is a wealth of information. But even with the insurance money, how can I put this place back together in time for the opening? That was our big night for business and The Smokehouse needs the money to pay bills. I don't want any more bags of…"

Elizabeth paled. Her eyes didn't seem to focus. She grabbed for Sunny, who took her arm. "Whoa. I think I have to sit down."

"It's the smoke. Reminds me of s'mores when you accidentally drop them in the fire. You know—marshmallows, chocolate, graham crackers all burning at the same time."

Sunny led Elizabeth to the porch, unscathed by the fire. "Hey, I remembered something."

"Wish you'd remembered fresh flowers and spring air." Elizabeth went green, turned her head to the side and got sick.

"That's it. I'm going for Doc. He's just over there." Sunny pointed up the street. "You could be—"

"Pregnant?" Elizabeth arched her eyebrow and managed a sheepish smile.

Sunny stopped midpoint. She sat down next to Elizabeth. "Wow. I didn't know. I mean, Gray never told me. Not that we share confidences." She smiled at Elizabeth. "That's wonderful news. Incredibly wonderful. So that's the doctor's appointment you're in town for. Do you want a drink of water?"

Elizabeth shook her head. "I have mints." She located one in her pocket, popped it in her mouth and closed her eyes for a second, letting the flavor calm her stomach. "I dropped off the legal paperwork to Ms. Rose for the flood-prevention project she's heading up. She just came back from her sister's. No one knows I'm pregnant, and that includes my dear husband."

"Hope he's a man who likes surprises."

"Tried to tell him yesterday as he mad-dashed through the house, going from an oil-rig meeting to a cattle-buying meeting. I said, 'Oh, Dillon, we're having a baby.' He must have thought I said *mashed potatoes and gravy,* because he asked if we were having roast beef with that."

Sunny chuckled. "Oh, boy."

"No way. This time it's *got* to be a girl."

The two women laughed. Elizabeth said, "Dillon can't run the Lazy K by himself, and it would be nice for him to know he has children before he starts paying college-tuition bills and wondering who it's for."

Sunny leaned back against the top step and billowed her gritty shirt to cool herself. She watched the firefighters gather up their equipment and load it back onto the truck.

"One thing's for sure. Gray getting elected mayor is more important than ever. Too bad I just killed his chances by accusing him of arson in front of half the town. Not a great campaign statement. Somehow I'll have to make things right." She kicked at a charred piece of wood lying on the ground. "But how?"

She looked back to The Smokehouse, more deserving of its name then ever. "And how am I ever going to get this place back together in six days?"

Elizabeth took her hand. "You'll think of something. You're that kind of woman."

Sunny smiled. "You're the one who's superwoman around here. Everyone in town admires you. Raising the twins with Dillon gone so much, assisting with town projects, even helping out at the bank when your dad needs you. And now you have another child on the way. I don't know how you do it."

"I have Dillon, so I'm happy."

Sunny patted her hand. As busy as Dillon was, he and Elizabeth were a great couple. They understood each other and got along. She and Gray could never be like that. They argued and disagreed and saw eye to eye on nothing.

GRAY ENTERED the charred saloon the next morning wondering how he and Sunny could argue and disagree and see eye to eye on nothing…but were so damn good together in the sack. He pulled up in front of her and glared. "You're totally nuts."

She put down a bucket of soapy water, suds sloshing onto the blackened floor. Her hair was tied back behind a red bandanna, left cheek smudged black, T-shirt more dirty than clean, and she was still attractive as hell. She had probably cost him the election, yet he still wanted to take her into his arms and kiss her. He was the one who was certifiably nuts!

"Where is everybody?"

"Getting supplies. And I don't want Jean near these fumes."

Gray nodded to the open door. "Mind explaining why you have a bedsheet fluttering out the upstairs window?"

"The one that says, Gray McBride Did Not Torch This Bar. I Apologize. I did it in Magic Marker."

"Did you realize there's a crowd in the street looking at it?"

"I'd hate that my efforts went unnoticed. I accused you in public—I needed to apologize the same way. And our arguing probably helped your campaign, since no one can think we're an item after such a ruckus."

"Are you *ever* unnoticed?"

"I'm a showgirl. Getting noticed is my business."

"Everybody's talking. Fluttering sheets from buildings are a rarity in Tranquility."

She sobered a bit. "So is accusing people of arson when they're innocent. As much as you want to win the election I know you wouldn't do anything underhanded to close the bar, and everyone in town understands that. You've lived here all your life. They appreciate the kind of guy you are. A skirt chaser, yes. An arsonist, no. Do you accept my apology, or what?"

"Yeah, I accept. And I didn't chase all that many skirts."

She pressed her lips together to keep from laughing and her expression seemed to clear the air between them.

He smiled, too. "All right, maybe I did. But that's

over." Mostly because when he looked at Sunny Kelly, he couldn't even think about any other woman. First time that had ever happened.

He took her hand, loving the feel of the two of them connected. "You know Elizabeth's pregnant?"

"Surely Dillon will want you to help out more now, so he can be home once in a while." She stepped closer, her eyes hopeful. "Now you don't have to worry about winning the election and being mayor, right?"

Gray stepped closer. He sighed. "Dillon just left on a two-day business trip. He's not letting up."

She touched Gray's cheek. "Thanks for putting up Smitty and Jean at the Lazy K."

He cupped her chin in his palm. Her skin was warm, smooth, soft. "Damn, I've missed you."

"We saw each other yesterday."

"Yesterday doesn't count." He wiped a smudge from her cheek. "You need a bath."

"What to help?"

Her eyes sparked hot like Texas lightning. Six dozed in the corner; a few insects buzzed about; the scent of burned wood lingered; morning sun slanted through the windows, making rectangles on the charred floor. He traced his thumb over her bottom lip; she didn't move.

Desire made his mouth dry. He brought his face to hers. He wanted to—no, needed to—kiss her, taste her, feel her lips on his, his tongue with hers.

"Hope I'm not interrupting anything, Gray," said Norm from the doorway. "Some clerk from over at the bank just dropped off this check." He waved it in the air. "It's from the town council. The guy said you needed it ASAP, and the council's pleased as punch you're going to make The Smokehouse part of the fire-house."

Norm shook his head and sighed, Sunny glared as she stepped away from him and Gray let out a deep breath. Things were bad yesterday and promised to get worse today. And he had no one to blame but himself.

Chapter Six

Gray watched Norm lay the check on the bar, give a little salute and walk away. Gray's eyes locked with Sunny's as she asked, "Okay, now what's going on?"

Dang. Why did the check get delivered now? Five minutes. All he'd needed was another measly five minutes and he'd have had his kiss.

"Don't get yourself into an uproar. I got this all worked out. It's the perfect answer for everyone. The town buys The Smokehouse before it gets condemned, you have your money and the town can fix The Smokehouse up as part of the firehouse."

He bent his head toward hers. Maybe now she'd kiss him. A great plan like this deserved a little reward, right?

Her eyes went from fire to ice and her voice raised an octave as she said, "Condemned?"

She glared and let go of him. *So much for that kiss.*

She put her hands on her hips. "You bum! You're in here sweet-talking me and all the while you're really here to buy The Smokehouse, *again*?"

"Look around. The place is totaled. You can't open by the rodeo weekend. You're bankrupt. I'm throwing you a lifeline here."

"Then why do I feel as if I got hit on the head with a brick?" She raised an eyebrow that said he was dog dirt. "I intend to have this bar in shape in five days for customers and for Smitty and Jane's wedding reception. Here's a little news flash for you. The Smokehouse is insured. I *can* fix it."

"Not in time for the Fourth, when everyone's in town and business is booming. You're mortgaged to the rafters. You have no money to carry you through the weeks you need to rebuild. Take the check. This place looks more like a real smokehouse than a bar and..."

Uh-oh. She stared straight ahead. Eyes bright. *Reader's Digest* brain on fast-forward. She asked, "What did you just say?"

"I said you should sell, dammit!"

"Not that. And you didn't say dammit. The other thing."

She pursed her lips...her very nice lips that he *still* wanted to kiss more than anything. "I said the place looks like a smokehouse."

She grinned. "That's it! You're a genius. First the Fireworks, now this. You should go into advertising and promotions."

"I'm a cowboy. I promote cows." And he sure didn't feel like a genius. He felt as if he'd just dug his own grave. "I take it back. Bet whatever I said it really wasn't that great. *Ah, hell.*"

She dusted her hands. "I've got five days to have this place ready to open and make my creditors happy. There's work to do."

"You have black-streaked floors, charred walls and beams and a sooty ceiling."

Sunny's eyes brightened more and she spread her arms to the ceiling, taking in the whole place. "I know. Isn't The Smokehouse perfect?"

"Your brain cooked along with the bar. Give it up."

"Give it up?" She laughed...a real laugh. Not some sarcastic cackle. She added, "Now, why would I do that when everything's terrific. And it's all because of you."

He ran his hand over his face. "Maybe I'm wrong. Think about that. I'm wrong lots of times. If you try to rebuild, it'll take a long time, and even longer to get your customers back and bring in new ones, and you'll walk away with nothing but a court date for bankruptcy—and that's if the place doesn't get condemned first. Either way, The Smokehouse and your plans are finished."

She folded her arms. "And if I sell, your election's in the bag."

He shoved his hands into his jean pockets and rocked back on his heels. "There is that. But you'll walk away with the money."

"Well, the rodeo better be one humdinger of a success for your sake, cowboy. You'll need luck and support to get elected. The Smokehouse is going to reopen on time and be a smashing success in spite of your attempt to sell me down the river. Just you wait and see what I do with this place."

He could wait, Gray decided as he watched Sunny do a confident sashay back into the bar. Rebuild? What a crazy idea.… But the woman had one dynamite sashay.

How could she put the place in shape in five days? How could he win the election if she didn't sell out and he make good on his campaign promise? He took off his hat. The brim stayed in his hand; the crown dropped to the ground. Terrific. It was ten o'clock in the morning and his day had already gone straight to hell.

SMITTY WALKED into The Smokehouse as Sunny picked up another can of varnish. "Well, there he is, Mr. Society, sleeping out at the Lazy K three nights in a row now."

She swallowed a sigh. *She'd* like to be the one sleeping out at the Lazy K. With Gray, even if she could wring his neck…his strong tanned neck, which led to his nice broad shoulders.

Smitty grinned. "That house is huge. Got lost twice just going to the bathroom. Jean's a big help to Elizabeth with her mother-in-law out of town, Dillon away on business and Elizabeth having bouts of morning sickness that last all day." Smitty pulled a face. "Feel damn sorry for Elizabeth."

Norm put another coat of red paint on the front door. "You and Jean will be so spoiled you won't want to move back to your apartment."

Smitty picked up a new light fixture for the ceiling. "You know what they say, there's no place like home."

He nodded at the charred timbers, walls and floor. "This here is home. Best I've ever had." He climbed the ladder.

Sunny wiped a varnish drip. "I hear the Freemonts' house is for sale. Nice little place. Good starter home. If we can get The Smokehouse going, maybe we can scrape together enough for a down payment and you and Jean can live there. Norm and Art can split the basement apartment in two and we can add another outside entrance to each for privacy. Auntie would have wanted it that way—I just know it."

The saloon went dead quiet. What happened to the chitchat? Sunny glanced up, to see all eyes turned her way. "What?"

Smitty licked his lips. "Jean and me have a house? With a yard for the baby?" His voice cracked and he licked his lips again.

Art blinked a few times, then cleared his throat. "Me and Norm having apartments?" He exchanged looks with Norm. "We're just broken-down cowpokes living in one-room walk-ups with the bathroom down the hall, scraping by from odd job to odd job." He swallowed. "You really mean it? An apartment?"

Sunny grinned. "Don't get all misty eyed. This is just business. If you live here, your rent will consist of mopping the barroom floor at night. I hate mopping the bar. And I'll have my own personal chef since Norm can make me Dagwoods once in a while and Art can fry up some of his onion rings when I feel my cholesterol start to slip below two hundred. But none of this will happen if we stand around all day yakking instead of working."

The men continued to stare at her as if she had three heads. "Yoo-hoo? Guys? Work? Does that sound familiar? Paint? Varnish? Finishing up The Smokehouse."

Art held up a black iron curtain rod. "Guess we…we better get a move on." He swallowed. "And, Sunny. Thanks."

Smitty and Norm nodded in agreement, appearing a bit bewildered, but in a good way. She went to Smitty and pointed to the ceiling. "The light goes there."

"Yeah. Right." He grinned and started fastening the fixture to the ceiling. "We're making good progress. With only replacing what's unsound, sanding away the loose charred parts and varnishing over the rest to make The Smokehouse look like its name, we should be done in two days easy."

He gave Sunny a slow grin. "Though I got to thinking about another little idea that could set us back a bit. Since half The Smokehouse is burned—" he nodded to the part where he stood "—and the other half isn't—" he nodded across the room "—why don't we have two sections? Use the rougher side for the pool table and Widow Maker, and the other half for tables and maybe a jukebox. The bar's in the middle and folks in both sections can use it. Put old cowboy memorabilia on the walls. I got some, and bet Art and Norm do, too."

Sunny slapped her palm to her forehead. "High concept and diversified clientele. Brilliant."

Smitty stroked his chin. "Actually, I was thinking all

kinds of people would like to have some fun here because it's different."

"We'll get the men and the women here along with cowboys and cowgirls. We have the perfect sandwich maker." She eyed Norm. "How'd you like to make lots of those Dagwoods? And Art could do lots of onion rings. Maybe invent a few new easy recipes after we get going? We can turn the storeroom into a small kitchen."

Art's eyes rounded. "Do I get one of those fancy white hats?"

Norm hooted. "It'll cover up the bald spot I've been fretting over."

"I think Suzzie Adams kind of likes your bald spot."

Sunny smiled. Norm had a girlfriend. *Good for Norm.* "Then I need to get to the hardware and grocery stores while you guys work on the construction. I'll pick up napkins and paper plates, and check on the flowers and cake for the wedding."

And since Gray was probably in town setting up for the rodeo, she'd check on him, too. Not that she'd ever want anything to do with him, of course. He was a class-A jerk for trying to close down The Smokehouse and condemn her property. But she could look. When it came to Gray she'd always look. What woman in her right mind wouldn't?

She stood, wiped sawdust from her jeans and pulled cash from the register. "I better pay up front. We don't need any more cement bags dropped on the bar. Good thing I found the last one and not Jean."

Smitty screwed in the light fixture. "What cement bags?"

"On the bar the other day. Stabbed straight through with a knife holding a note saying pay up. Guess me being a showgirl from Reno who owns this bar doesn't make creditors feel all warm and fuzzy with confidence. I can understand that."

She picked up more flyers for the opening of The Smokehouse, then headed for the door. She stopped with her hand on the doorknob, all three men staring at her wide-eyed for the second time this morning. "Now what?"

Smitty cleared his throat. "Uh, I don't know how they do things in Reno, but stabbed cement bags are not a usual occurrence in Tranquility."

"It was just a hint to pay some bills...that weren't even due yet and..." A shiver snaked up her spine.

Norm waved his hand over the room. "Kids causing fires isn't common, either...especially at a bar. Brush and barn fires, maybe, but not this. And now there's the bag-of-cement thing to go along with it." He shook his head. "Something's up and it ain't good."

Sunny bit her bottom lip. "You think the cement bag and the fire are connected? Why? How? What the heck should I do about it?"

Norm raked his sandy hair. "It's what should *we* do, since we're all in this together. We can't tell the sheriff what's going on because he'll tell his wife and our grand opening will look like a ghost town if people think The Smokehouse isn't safe."

Art gazed through the front window. "We need to keep an eye out. I don't think whoever did this will torch the bar again, but they could try something else. We'll make sure one of us is always here during the day. We can split the shifts at night so we can all catch a little sleep."

She looked from one to the other. "Any of you have enemies?"

Norm's eyes narrowed. "I don't think it's us. It's you. The cement was left on *your* bar. They could have gotten to us some other time." He nodded at Smitty. "Have Jean stay out at the Lazy K till we get this figured out."

Sunny held her hands out, palms up. "But I'm an outsider. I don't know anyone here except superficially. Why would someone have it in for me?"

Smitty gave her a thin-lipped smile. "Maybe someone doesn't like rhinestones and feathers. Just stay out of back alleys, okay?"

Sunny closed the door behind her and headed for Nails to Pails Hardware. *This is crazy.* How could anything bad, really bad, happen in a place called Tranquility? Though Leroy hadn't found the kids who'd started the fire. Maybe the cement bag and the fire were a coincidence. Yeah, and maybe roosters laid eggs.

She tacked the flyers to telephone poles as she made her way down one tree-lined street and across to another. The sound of hammering, powers saws and the smell of cut wood hung in the summer air as she walked past neat houses. Roses cascaded over picket fences; porch swings stirred in the gentle breeze; sprinklers tossed water droplets skyward, making them sparkle like diamonds against the clear blue Texas sky. Bet Reno wasn't like this.

When she turned onto Main, a half-built rodeo ring and set of bleachers sat smack in the middle of the intersection. Bet Reno wasn't like this, either. She walked to the corral, stepped over a bale of hay and then up onto the first rung of the metal gate and began to pass out flyers to the hardworking cowboys who may have forgotten to sign up for events. Discreetly she kept an eye out for Gray. Elizabeth stepped up beside her and took a handful of flyers to pass out.

Sunny asked, "What are you doing in town so early in the morning?"

"Trying not to get sick." She flashed Sunny a lopsided smile. "And I'm helping Ms. Rose line up women volunteers for the quilt and pie contests and the ice-cream social and the taffy pull. Bring in a little more revenue and give people something to do between the rodeo and the fireworks."

"Doesn't it seem to you that the women do all the family stuff around here? The guys work and only the women take care of the family."

Elizabeth shrugged. "That's the way it's always been. Tranquility is kind of old-fashioned, I guess. Women stay at home. Guys go off to work."

"Seems to me they just go off, period."

"Yeah, I guess they do. But since we *are* old-fashioned, we make it a point of having great fireworks on the Fourth of July. And this year we'll have a rodeo, too. Should go a long way to get Gray elected. He's working hard enough."

"He thinks Dillon needs his help at the Lazy K now more than ever, with you being pregnant and all."

Elizabeth sighed. "Wish he'd just stand up to Dillon and take what's his."

Sunny shook her head. "Gray's not about to take anything. He feels he owes Dillon for raising him and saving the ranch. He's not going to square off against his brother." She looked around. "Where are the twins?"

"With Jean. Don't know what I'd do without her. She's walking them up to The Smokehouse. She's missing Smitty." Elizabeth sighed. "Now there's a feeling I can relate to. Dillon's home less and less."

She handed a flyer to a young cowboy as he passed by. "Think the prime grade-A herd of maleness around here is stripped to the waist to keep cool, or to keep the womenfolk in Tranquility hot as spit on a griddle?"

Sunny chuckled. "Married women aren't supposed to notice such things."

"Honey, I'm pregnant, not dead."

She liked being with Elizabeth, who was smart, spunky, civic-minded, a great mom. And that wasn't just Sunny's opinion. Everybody in town thought so, too. "Catch that cowboy hoisting bales of hay." She nodded to the far side of the ring. "I doubt if there's a finer hunk of man in the whole U.S.A., except for…"

"Gray?" Elizabeth finished with a raised eyebrow

while Sunny couldn't believe what she herself had nearly said out loud.

"That *exception*," Elizabeth continued with a twinkle in her eye, "is around back setting up holding pens and chutes for the cattle, if you want to check him out." She laughed. "You haven't seen him in a while, have you?"

"It shows?"

"You're blushing."

Sunny handed out another flyer. "It's the heat. Gray's present mission in life is *still* to close The Smokehouse and enlarge the firehouse. We're not on speaking terms—more like arguing terms. And even if we weren't, we couldn't socialize, because Gray's convincing everyone he's given up his loose-and-reckless ways." She pointed a finger at herself. "That would be me, a Reno showgirl with amnesia who owns a cowboy bar. Not the best image for a campaign, especially in a town where women mind hearth and home, and men mind the business."

Elizabeth chuckled. "You really believe that little speech you just made?"

Sunny grinned. "I'm trying really hard to." She shouldn't be here to see Gray. What a stupid idea. Like waving a candy bar in front of a diabetic. "I better go before he shows up and my well-thought-out speech takes another hit."

She turned her head to check where to step, and came face-to-face with Gray. Shirt off, narrow waist hugged by low-slung dusty jeans. His tanned skin glistened with perspiration, showing off his great build even more. A real cowboy. She remembered making love with him, her hands on him…his on her. She fanned herself with the rest of the flyers. "It must be over a hundred degrees out here. How'd it get so hot?"

He gave her a tight smile. "Yeah, me, too."

Her heart raced, her insides flipped, her knees weakened. *Don't drool! Say something, anything, to keep from staring.* "How are the booths for the contest?"

Not brilliant, but considering she had weak knees, it could have been worse…like, *Gray, you big stud, make love to me now and to heck with the election. That* would have been a lot worse!

Gray stroked his chin. "We have enough volunteers, but Doc's getting a little testy. Even though Ms. Rose is back, they're not seeing each other. He put the entire cattleman's association on a vegetarian diet and chased Leroy out of Doris's Doughnuts. He's her best customer. He better give Ms. Rose's apple pie the blue ribbon so we can get those two together."

He took off his hat, duct tape holding it together, and wiped his forehead with the back of his arm. "Don't know who's crankier—Doc or the people he runs into."

She considered the sun-bleached chest hair trailing down his middle and disappearing beneath the waistband to… *She had to get out of here.*

"I've…I've got to pick up supplies at the hardware store, then check on the wedding cake and flowers for Smitty and Jane's wedding tomorrow." *And cool off!*

She stuffed the remaining flyers in Gray's hand.

"See you in Merryweather's chambers for the event. Four o'clock sharp. Don't be late, and don't forget the groom."

She crossed the street. How could she fall for a guy who wanted to tear down the thing she wanted most to save? Somehow she had to get over Gray McBride.

But by midnight, as she sat on the front steps of The Smokehouse with a baseball bat across her lap, she still didn't know how to get over him. She didn't have one clue, because whenever she thought about Gray, getting rid of him was the last thing on her mind—and she thought about him a lot.

Maybe Coke and Oreos would help her come up with a plan. A sugar high to stimulate the brain and curb her sex drive. Could sugar do that? Maybe not, but it would keep her awake for the next two hours. She snagged the treats from upstairs, then reclaimed her place on the porch. She popped the Coke and poked a hole in the pack of Oreos. She fed Six a cookie, took one for herself, twisted it apart and scraped the white icing with her index finger and licked it. At the moment everything was quiet. Most of the men in Tranquility were either at the cattlemen's meeting or playing poker over at Lucky Tanner's. Life was good, predictable…except for the thunking noise behind The Smokehouse.

So much for predictable. Another cement delivery? Six's ears perked up; his tail stopped wagging. She shoved the rest of the cookie into her mouth—courage food—and gripped the bat. She'd agreed to call Art or

Norm if she heard anything, *anything* at all. But this could very well be a dog of the other gender paying a late-night call to seduce Six. The hussy!

"Good thing we're getting your jets cooled next week," she said around a mouthful of crumbs. "Come on."

She picked up a flashlight and tippy-toed around the back of the saloon. A streetlight on the next block illuminated part of the alley. A truck. A guy…a big guy carrying stuff. "Get him, Six."

Six sat, wagged his tail and barked. *Hey, at least he barked.* Sunny charged the man with her bat drawn, only to have it whipped out of her hand and tossed to the ground. "What the hell are you doing?" said Gray.

"What the hell am *I* doing?" Her heart raced, and adrenaline made her see double. Showgirl–security guard wasn't a great mix. "Me? This is still my bar. You're the one who doesn't belong here, who scared me half to death and—"

"Will you hush? You'll wake everybody in the whole blasted town. It's after midnight."

"I will not hush until you tell me what you're doing here at this hour and—"

He kissed her, shutting her up and making her angrier…for about two seconds. Then she kissed him back.

Didn't she have any willpower at all when it came to Gray McBride? He deepened the kiss, his hands gently framing her face. For her, willpower and Gray did not belong in the same sentence. But she had to try.

She pulled out of his embrace, then berated herself for trying so hard. "Why *are* you here?"

He gave her a sincere smile, not the kind wanting to prove something, but the kind that said he was glad to be with her. "I needed that kiss...and hoped maybe you did, too."

She gave him a dismissive shrug. "A little."

He arched his eyebrow.

Her shrug collapsed. "Okay, a lot." Owning up to this was not a great beginning to getting him out of her brain. "But why *else* are you here? It's about the saloon again, isn't it?"

He shoved his hat to the back of his head, the street-light casting shadows over his face. "Yeah, it's about the saloon."

"I knew it." She threw her hands in the air. "You've got some other devious plan cooked up to get me to sell the place. Well, you're wasting your time."

He nodded at the truck. "These are building materials left over from the rodeo. Thought you might be able to use it for the apartments you're building for Norm and Art. The whole town's talking about it."

"And you brought this wood now? Why?"

He planted his hands on his hips and exhaled. After studying the ground for a second, he said, "Okay, I'm so damn tired of all this sneaking-around stuff, I'll tell you why. Because I couldn't sleep. Because coming here got me closer to you for a few minutes. I didn't plan on the kiss, but I'm damn glad it happened. I miss you like mad, hate that we fight more than make love.

Wanted to sneak a peek inside the saloon, since you have the windows papered over, and I admire you for what you're doing for Smitty, Jean, Art and Norm. There, is that good enough for you?"

She stared at him, dumbfounded. "You…you admire me?"

He did a wide grin, his teeth white against the night. "Just wish my campaign wasn't getting trampled in the path of all your good deeds."

"They're all for Auntie. It's what she would have wanted, I just know it. I'd like to think she was proud of me."

"None of us in town even knew about you till she died. It's hard to imagine you two being so close."

"I don't know because I can't remember, but I have a feeling of gratitude I can't shake." Sunny ran her hand through her hair. "I like what I'm doing, but I'd hate for you to lose the election because of it."

"I've been thinking about that and I have an idea."

"Your last great idea was getting The Smokehouse condemned."

"I have another plan. If the rodeo brings in enough revenue, we can build another fire station. We can have two smaller fire stations. I can get the town council to go for that, maybe."

"Let me get this straight. You mean you're not going to try anything else to close down The Smokehouse because I made good with some venture capital and helped Smitty, Jean, Norm and Art?"

His eyes darkened and he took her in his arms. She

felt warm and wonderful and incredibly happy. "No. I have other reasons."

His mouth covered hers, and now he kissed her as if his life depended on it. "You *are* gorgeous and sexy and kind and understanding and hardworking…and I'm falling for you."

HE COULDN'T BELIEVE he had Sunny in his arms and was kissing her, loving the way she felt against him. He'd wanted this since they'd made love on the pool table, had stayed awake nights thinking about it, and now here she was, more wonderful than ever. She pulled her head back and gazed into his eyes and he felt the whole world stop.

"What time is it?"

If she'd slapped him upside the head with a dead carp he couldn't have been more surprised. "Time?"

She took his hand from around her waist and held up his watch to the streetlight. "We have to leave."

"What's going on?"

She bent down and picked up the bat. "While I'm making out with you here, there could be someone inside the bar. I better check."

She started back down the walk and he snagged her arm. "Why would someone be in the saloon?" He nodded at the bat. "Why are you outside at midnight with a Louisville Slugger for company? Batting practice?"

"Only if you're a bad guy. But you're not, so don't worry about it." She kissed him again. "Go home."

Now fully awake, all thoughts of holding her gone,

he looked her right in the eyes…her big green eyes that mesmerized him. "What bad guy? What are you talking about?" Why couldn't he just fall for an ordinary woman who knitted and cooked, instead of one who chased bad guys with bats?

She swatted a mosquito. "Since the fire, we're making sure nothing else happens to the bar."

"Where are Smitty, Norm and Art?"

She set her chin stubbornly. "You're not going to like this, I just know it. So try to get a grip, okay?" She pulled in a deep breath. "It's my turn to watch The Smokehouse for the next two hours. Except I'm not doing a very good job watching if I'm making out with you." She smiled and stroked his cheek. "I'm not complaining, mind you. But I have to get to work. I can handle this. *Go home.*"

He kept hold of her arm, narrowed his eyes and gave her a no-nonsense look. "Define *this.*"

She rolled her eyes. "A bag of cement on the bar and no one knows where it came from."

"And?"

More eye rolling. "And it had a hole in it…from a knife…with a note telling me to pay up."

He let go of her arm and clenched his hands. His blood pressure skyrocketed. Dots danced before his eyes. *"What the hell? Why didn't you tell me before now? Why didn't Art or Smitty or Norm?"*

"Until five minutes ago you and I weren't exactly on the same page where The Smokehouse was concerned. Don't go getting your boxers in a bunch. It's probably nothing, just some teenagers having fun. But we—Norm, Art and me—decided to keep watch. Smitty's with Jean, but I'm to call Norm and Art on this handy-dandy cell phone—" she pulled it from her jean pocket and waved it at him "—and tell them if there was any trouble at all."

"And they went along with this cockamamy idea?"

She grinned. "I'm the boss. Plus, I have Six to protect me."

Gray patted Six as he wagged his tail and slobbered on his boot. Not exactly the marines. "We do have a sheriff in this town, you know."

"Who's married to Ms. Blabbermouth U.S.A. We need to keep things uncomplicated for the saloon opening to be a success." She turned and he trailed after her.

"Your truck's back there," she said, hitching her chin at the alley. "Art and Norm are a phone call away."

"We *are* on the same page of The Smokehouse. You are not *my* boss, so you can get used to me being with you till the next shift shows up."

"You can't."

He gave her his best just-watch-me look.

She faced him and kissed him. "I'm really enjoying you wanting to protect me and all, and you'd probably do it if we were mortal enemies because that's the way you are. But us sitting on the front porch together like Ma and Pa on a hot summer's night is not the image you want right now." She gave *him* a knowing look. "You have an election to win?"

He kicked a rock across the sidewalk. "I'm not leaving. I'll get my truck and park on Oak. I can see The Smokehouse from the corner."

"What if Leroy shows? What are you going to tell him? I don't want him in on this cement thing. His wife will get involved and the opening will be doomed."

"I'll tell Leroy I'm sleeping off a few too many beers. He'll buy that, and it's not something that will kill my election." He snagged her in his arms and kissed her hard. Reluctantly he let he go, kissed her nose and her cheek and headed back to the truck, grumbling swearwords about the election, his brother, the town and all things keeping him from Sunny Kelly.

TWO DAYS LATER Sunny held Jean's hand as they got out of Doc's minivan, waved a cheery goodbye, then walked up the stone steps of the Tranquility courthouse. Sunlight played in the trees; white puffy clouds hung in a perfect blue sky. Sunny smiled. "A wonderful day to get married…then again, it could be snowing and hailing golf balls and it would be a wonderful day for you and Smitty to marry."

Jean licked her bottom lip and fiddled with her bouquet of pink roses and baby's breath. "What if he isn't here?"

"Now why would that happen?"

"What if Smitty backs out? What if he doesn't want to marry me after all and has second thoughts?"

Sunny ushered Jean to the side of the steps shaded by a big oak. "Smitty *will* be here. You know how he worked like mad to finish up The Smokehouse for today, and it wasn't just for the grand opening. Got the cake and flowers himself early this morning before he went out to the Lazy K to get dressed with Gray. Wild horses couldn't keep Smitty from you. He's as excited as you are about getting married. Who can blame him?" She patted Jean's hand. "You're beautiful and radiant and—"

"Pregnant with another man's baby." She rubbed her rounded middle under her lovely cream linen suit. "What if Smitty decides this is a bad idea?"

"He won't. He knows a real father is the one who raises the child. Smitty loves you with all his heart, just as you love him. I envy you. What you and Smitty have is special."

She held Jean's hand and led her through the double wooden doors, into the cool hallway. Sunny meant what she'd said about envying Jean. She had a loving husband, a baby on the way, a bright future. Who could ask for more? She nudged Jean. "Smile. It's your wedding day."

But Jean continued to nibble her bottom lip and twist the satin ribbons on the bouquet till the two of them reached Judge Merryweather's chambers at the end of the hall. Jean paled. Sunny took her arm and said, "Smitty's probably waiting for you on the other side of that door."

"You think?"

"Absolutely." Sunny prayed she was right. "It's going to be fine. Great. Wonderful."

As they entered, Judge Merryweather held out his

hand to Jean in greeting. "What a beautiful bride. Congratulations, my dear."

Jean paled a bit more as she glanced around. "Smitty's not here?"

The judge checked his watch. "It's just four now. The groom seems to be running a little late."

Sunny nodded and continued smiling while mentally throwing darts at Gray and Smitty. *Where the heck were they?* "Smitty had to come in from the Lazy K. Gray McBride's the best man."

Judge Merryweather's eyes shot open wide. "Now, there's a guy who will always be the best man and never the groom. Settling down is the last thing on his mind."

Sunny considered that. The judge was right. *Gray* and *settling down* didn't mix. He might be falling for her…but what exactly did that mean, and just how many other women had Gray fallen for? She and Gray had no future together, with the election and being mayor and her owning the saloon. And one of these days she'd have to go back to Reno. What surprises waited for her there? She and Gray were completely mismatched, all wrong for each other, had nothing in common…so why was she falling for him, too?

The judge nodded at a small leather couch. "Why don't you ladies sit down."

He gave Jean a reassuring smile that didn't quite meet his eyes as he glanced at her rounded middle. "Grooms are late. This happens. Nothing to worry about." He looked at the door, checked his watch again and said in a tighter voice, "Nothing at all."

Chapter Seven

The grandfather clock in the judge's chambers ticked off the minutes. Jean fidgeted, Merryweather paced and Sunny eyed the gavel on the big mahogany desk as the perfect instrument to beat Smitty and Gray over the head with when they finally *did* show up. *How could they do this to Jean?*

Sunny took Jean's hand. "He'll be here. *They'll* be here. I know it."

Judge Merryweather stopped and inhaled a deep breath. "I hate to do this, but I have another ceremony over in Springside at five and we're running out of time here. We can simply reschedule." He patted Jean's shoulder. "I'm sure your young man will show up. He's probably had car trouble…or some other kind of trouble."

The judge shifted from foot to foot. "You're welcome to stay for a few minutes. My assistant will lock up after you're…gone." He cleared his throat and left, the door closing with an ominous click behind him.

Sunny stooped in front of Jean and gazed into her

watery eyes. "You know Smitty. He's not like this. He would never leave you. There's got to be some explanation."

Jean smiled through her tears. "Yeah, it's called reaching for the moon when you have no business reaching at all."

Just then, the door burst open and Gray and Smitty walked in, both men looking as if they'd been dragged behind a herd of buffalo. Smudged shirts, string ties askew, mangled suit jackets, scuffed boots, dirty faces.

They escorted Judge Merryweather between them. Gray said, "Guess who we found in the hall, and just when we needed a judge for a wedding. Imagine that."

Jean stood, wiping tears from her eyes. Smitty froze. "You're crying? I can't believe I made you cry on our wedding day."

Jean straightened her shoulders and held her head high. "Of course you didn't. Just got something in my eye is all." She grinned and blushed, her face bright with happiness as she took in Smitty. "Oh, my. You're so handsome in your suit. And you have new boots and everything."

Gray and Sunny exchanged looks. Handsome? He and Smitty resembled something the cat chased and caught. Love was truly blind. Sunny said, "What happened?"

Merryweather stood in front of his desk. "You can all catch up later." He smoothed back his hair and drew himself up tall, appearing very judgelike. He removed a black book from his vest pocket. "We have two people who very much want to get married and we've wasted enough time already."

"Amen to that," Smitty said as he hooked Jean's arm through his and they took their places in front of the judge. The happy couple exchanged vows and rings and a kiss and then another kiss. Merryweather placed his arms around them and introduced them as husband and wife.

Jean beamed as she eyed the simple gold band on her finger. "I can't believe it." She turned her attention and loving gaze to her new husband. "Who would have thought that someday I'd be Mrs. Smitty?"

Smitty kissed her cheek. "I did. Least I hoped and prayed it would happen."

The judge left in a rush and the bridal party ambled down the main hall of the courthouse. "Okay," Sunny asked. "What happened to make you two late? And it better be good."

Smitty laughed. "Car trouble."

"More like bull trouble that came after the car trouble," Gray said. He draped his big arm around her, then took it away as if remembering her admonition— *nothing between them in pubic to jeopardize the election.* "We ran out of gas, cut across Miller's south field to borrow some time and met up with Bone Crusher."

Jean gasped and looked at Smitty. "Are you hurt?"

He laughed harder. "Nope. We ran like hell and dived over the fence to escape. Just like back in my rodeo days."

Sunny poked Gray in the ribs and his eyes widened. "What was that for?"

"Running out of gas in the first place." *And nearly giving me a heart attack.*

GRAY STRAIGHTENED his shoulders and fought to keep his hands to himself when he'd much rather have them on Sunny, holding her hand or just touching her in any way. "Hey, I've been busy with the rodeo. I can't think of everything." *Because I keep thinking of you.*

Sunny was stunning in her blue suit that matched the sky. Her eyes danced with happiness and her cheeks held a healthy glow of excitement. How could anyone resist Sunny Kelly? He couldn't. Running out of gas wasn't the only thing he'd screwed up in the past three days. The reason he had extra wood to deliver to The Smokehouse was that he'd cut a lot of boards the wrong length.

"Wow," Smitty said as they opened the front doors of the courthouse. "What a great day." He swung Jean up into his arms. "I want to carry you over the threshold."

She giggled, "That's four blocks away."

He kissed her, then kissed her again. "I need practice." Laughing, he took off down the street, his bride cradled proudly in his arms.

Gray said, "Those two are going to be okay. More than okay. Makes me believe in love everlasting." Gray wanted to hold Sunny the way Smitty held Jean. Instead, Gray placed his hand on Sunny's shoulder, a damn poor substitute. "It's a good marriage for two people who'd fought some pretty tough battles and won."

She gave him a sincere smile. "Good guys don't finish last…in love or elections. You're going to be okay, too, Gray McBride."

They ambled toward The Smokehouse, following the newlyweds. Gray nodded at Jean and Smitty. "I wonder if they know there are other people on the planet?"

She chuckled. "Of course not." She drew a deep breath. "Will people assume we're a couple since we're together like this? With the election next week we can't take any chances."

He shook his head. "Everybody knows we stood up for Smitty and Jean. We just look like two people going home from an afternoon wedding, following the bride and groom."

She glanced around. "Where is everybody? There doesn't seem to be all that many people around. The houses are decorated with red, white and blue everything, but nobody's out. Kind of strange for the day before the holiday, isn't it? Thought there'd be more festivities."

"There're plenty of festivities. They're all at The Smokehouse."

She stopped in the middle of the sidewalk. "Huh?"

He leaned casually against a telephone pole and stuck his hands in his pockets to keep from tucking a wayward strand of silky gold hair behind her ear. "The

Smokehouse is the talk of the town since you put that paper over the windows and won't let anyone see inside. Everybody's dying of curiosity to know what's going on in there. Put that together with Smitty and Jean's wedding reception and the lure of free beer and Norm's Dagwoods and Art's onion rings and you pretty much can figure where the festivities are."

Her eyes widened. "I...we can't feed all those people."

"You'll do the best you can and everyone will help and it'll be one hell of a good time. That's the way things are in Tranquility." He kissed her on the nose because he simply had to kiss her somewhere and that seemed the most innocent place. *Except he did not want to be innocent with Sunny Kelly.* "I bet if you listen real hard you can hear the music and hubbub from The Smokehouse all the way here."

"Two blocks?"

"Consider yourself a success, Showgirl Sunny. The Smokehouse is having a really grand opening." He barely got the words out before she ran off, blue skirt flying as she called over her shoulder, "I have to go."

He let her reach The Smokehouse before him—best to have as little connection with her as possible. *Damn,* he hated that. Hated it more all the time, and seeing Smitty and Jean together and happy made him feel worse. The woman he wanted in his life was completely off-limits. If it wasn't for Dillon and Elizabeth, Mom and the boys, he'd chase after Sunny Kelly. But what would he do once he caught her? She was more to him than a fling. But what?

Sunny beat him to the saloon by a half block and he watched her laugh and greet her way though the crowd spilling out onto the porch and sidewalk. Her new friends Maxine and Hal, Connie and Dixon, Bea, Gus, Tommy Lee and the others laughed, pointed to the inside of The Smokehouse and smiled hugely. Guess the place was okay by them. Everyone liked Sunny. Most people liked him. The problem was Sunny and him together. She was too much like the sassy, flirty gals he used to chase. Thing was, he never cared about them the way he cared for Sunny Kelly.

Sunny disappeared inside, and Gray took in the scene. Art and Norm passing out sandwiches and beers and onion rings. Kenny Rogers singing about love keeping people together. The porch table overflowing with wedding gifts.

One woman, one idea, one hell of a day. No one made things happen like Sunny. Smitty came up to him and placed a long neck in his hand. "Thanks for introducing me to Jean."

Gray clinked his bottle to Smitty's. "To Jean." They took a swig and Gray said, "I didn't think you'd want to go far with the baby due pretty soon, so I made arrangements for you and Jean to spend the next few nights at the Corner Stone Inn over by the Mill Pond Restaurant. And they're expecting you for dinner each evening—on me."

Smitty wagged his head. "I don't know how to thank you."

Gray grinned. "You just did." He shrugged. "You can do me a favor, though."

Smitty nodded. "Don't worry about a thing. Art, Norm and I are watching over Sunny. We'll keep her safe for you."

"How'd you know about me and…"

Smitty laughed. "Hell, Gray, all anyone has to do is look at you two when you're within ten feet of each other and watch the sparks fly."

"Think anyone else notices?"

"Most don't see you together all that much. Damn shame this town doesn't realize Sunny isn't just another pretty face and high-spirited woman for you like the other gals, that she's someone special."

"I'm supposed to be a changed man, and being with a gorgeous saloon owner-Reno showgirl doesn't make me looked changed at all."

"But you are. Like Jean says, you are once and for all *off the market*."

Gray sloshed his beer. *Off the market?* Him? Nah. He gave a chuckle. "I wouldn't go so far as to say that."

Smitty grinned like a dog eyeing dinner. "You will, old buddy. You will."

Before Gray could think of another disclaimer—mostly because everything he came up with sounded damn feeble—Smitty asked, "I wonder if all these good folks will stay around once the free beer turns into paying beer?"

Gray slapped Smitty on the back. "This crew's just

getting warmed up. It's going to be a long profitable night at The Smokehouse. Sure wish I could hang around, but I have cattle to truck in for tomorrow, or there won't be a rodeo or revenue and I can kiss being mayor goodbye."

"You doing some bull riding?"

Gray nodded. "We're bringing in some of ours, and Miller's lending us Bone Crusher. Should be one hell of an event."

"If you survive."

SUNNY SAID GOOD-NIGHT to two more couples as they headed out the saloon door. The jukebox played an Elvis tune about rocking in jail and the din from the cowboy section dropped a few decibels as empty tables appeared here and there. She handed Art a full tray of bottles. "Well, we did it."

He laughed as he took the tray and handed her an empty one. "By golly, I think we did. And I don't know about you, but I'm bushed."

She nodded at the cowboys shooting pool. "Who are the newcomers? They're getting a late start on the fun."

"Boys from the Lazy K. Brought in the cattle with Gray for the rodeo tomorrow. I'm guessing he's cow-sitting and letting his boys kick up their heels a bit."

Sunny felt instantly alert. Gray? Did Art mention Gray? "That's…interesting."

"You want me to find you an escort so you can visit Mr. Interesting? Norm and I have to mind the store, but I'm sure I can get someone to walk with you." He nodded toward the jukebox. "Doc and Ms. Rose have been sitting there all night. Bet they'd walk with you down to the pens and—"

She waved away his words as if shooing a pesky fly. "I wouldn't interrupt Doc and Ms. Rose for anything. Besides, did I say I was going anywhere?"

"You didn't have to. I know that look in your eye whenever Gray's around."

"You have an overactive imagination." She snagged some empty long necks as Art laughed. He flirted with a cute little redhead as Sunny inched her way toward the storeroom. She put down the empties, untied her apron, left both by the back door, then closed it silently behind her. She headed for the town square.

There wasn't any need to have someone with her. With so much going on in town, nothing would happen to her and she really wanted to see Gray. She missed him. Their short time together at the wedding made her want to see him more. *Would she ever get enough of Gray McBride?*

Heat and humidity saturated the night. A nearly full moon lit the sky; streetlight filtered through the trees. Flags hung limp on their poles, as if resting up for the big celebration tomorrow. Red, white and blue bunting decorated fences and storefronts. Lawn chairs and blankets dotted the curbs, holding the best places to view tomorrow's parade of homemade floats and the high-school band. Fourth of July comes to Texas.

If she had to have amnesia, Tranquility was the place to have it—pretty town, terrific folks, new friends…and Gray. She'd never forget Gray. But obviously people had forgotten her. No one from Reno had come looking for her. Maybe she'd be better off if her memory never returned. But if it did, then what?

She turned down Oak, passed Snicker Doodle Candies and Cards— And got jerked into a dark alley and plastered hard against the side of the wooden building by a body that felt like a steamroller, not that she actually knew what a steamroller felt like, but she was getting the idea real fast. She could barely breathe. Maybe because a hand covered her mouth.

"You had a profitable night, girlie-girl," said a voice laced with beer breath.

It was one thing to scare her to death, another to make her gag. She wanted to offer him a mint, but it didn't seem appropriate. A mint? Funny how the mind works when you're terrified.

"Boss says you've got till the end of the week to pay up or else."

The guy ran off down the alley. She stumbled out to the sidewalk and collapsed into one of the lawn chairs, her heart nearing explosion level. She put her head between her legs to keep from passing straight out. She should sterilize her mouth where he'd put his hand. *Blah.*

Who the heck was that? A baseball cap sporting a cement-truck logo had shadowed his face, hiding his features. She sat up and took a deep steadying breath. None of this made sense. *Pay who?* Gray couldn't help her figure this out because he'd then risk the election to be with her and protect her. As for the other men in her life, Smitty was on his honeymoon and Art and Norm had their hands full keeping a new business afloat and didn't need to baby-sit her. A dog. She needed a big dog.

She had a big dog. Look where that had gotten her—squashed against a building. She should get out of here before the cement guy returned. She took off in a dead run and ran until she heard the soft moo of cows and saw Gray twirling a lasso by the cattle pens, showing one of the town kids how to snag a pole. She suddenly felt completely safe. Nothing would happen to her now. Gray would throw himself in traffic for her…and she for him. She slowed to a walk, trying to catch her breath and letting her fear fade away.

"Sunny?" Gray said. He motioned her over. "Thought you had a saloon to run."

"Came to visit the cows like everybody else." She grinned at the boy. Even at midnight people were still out and about. A rodeo at the intersection of Oak and Main didn't happen every day. "Norm said you were cow-sitting." She watched the boy try his hand.

"Not bad," Gray said to the kid. Then to Sunny, "Did Norm walk you down?"

Uh-oh. She did not want to start World War Three over her walking alone. She didn't want to think about the creepy guy with the cement truck on his hat who smelled like a brewery. "Not Norm. But I didn't walk down alone." Hey, it wasn't a lie; she'd had company.

That creepy guy was company, though probably not what Gray had in mind.

Before he asked more nosy questions she didn't feel like answering, she picked up another rope from a hay bale. "I should learn how to do this roping thing. If a cowboy gets out of control at The Smokehouse I can throw a rope around him and tie him up."

The boy laughed, thanked Gray and went to his father, who was standing by one of the pens, talking to neighbors.

Gray took the rope from her hands. "Let me give you some pointers. It's all in the wrist."

He stepped back a ways, opened the lasso, swung it over his head and neatly sent it over her. He smiled wickedly. "You never know when a good rope will get you exactly what you want."

The heated look drove the air right out of her lungs. This was not supposed to be a sexual encounter, just a diversion from the truth. "Okay, my turn." She took off the lasso and he handed her the rest of the rope. Her fingers brushed his, their gazes connected, her insides tightened with wanting him. The diversion was turning into a lot more than she'd bargained for.

She twirled the lasso and it tangled around her head…her waist, her knees. But on the seventh try, she wobbled one over Gray's head. She tugged on the rope, cinching his arms to his body.

"Is this how you intend to control misbehaving cowboys?"

"Depends on the cowboy." He was such a terrific

cowboy. "And right now I'd like to do a little misbehaving."

Had she really said that in public? Not a great idea, even though no one seemed to be listening except the cows. "I want to kiss you so bad I can taste it. If I was blindfolded and kissed a dozen men all lined up in a row, I'd know when I kissed you."

He tugged on the rope. Step by step bringing her closer to him. His brown eyes dark and hungry…and not for dinner. "I don't want to hear about you kissing a dozen men."

Her heart kicked up a notch. A touch of passion sparked in his eyes. She lifted the rope over his muscular chest, broad shoulders, determined chin and wonderful lips and eyes. She touched a scar at his hairline. "What happened here? Some other knock-down-drag-out fight with the Barns brothers?"

"Slider happened."

"Don't know any Slider in Tranquility."

"Pocatello, Idaho." Her fingers brushed against his hair, and hot lust snapped through her like the crack of a whip. "Sunny?"

"What happened in Iowa?"

"Idaho. Slider's a bull. Like the ones in that pen." He nodded. "Dynamite, Slingshot, Bone Crusher. I rode Slider. He wasn't thrilled with the idea."

The hair on the back of her neck stood straight up and she stepped back. "You rode one of…*them*?" She jabbed an accusing finger at the bullpen. "That's crazy." She ran her hand through her hair. "I mean… I knew you rode bulls, but until I actually *saw* the bulls up close and personal… This is way too personal. You're not going to ride any of these guys tomorrow? Are you?"

His eyes brightened. "Can't wait. Haven't done any bull riding in years." He gave her a cocky smile. "Just watch me tomorrow. You'll love it."

"No, I won't. I won't love any part of it." Her fists tightened. "Bulls are not made for riding. Why do you think they kick and snarl when someone's on their back, Gray? There's a message here. They have 'Come near me and get your head broken' written all over them."

He grinned mischievously. "You're worried about me?"

Yikes. What should she say to that? If she told the truth—that she was worried to hell and back about him—it would take their relationship to another level. Two people truly caring for each other was *not* a good thing for a relationship going nowhere. Besides, too many people milling about were suddenly more interested in what they were saying than in the cattle. "Anyone who rides a bull is totally insane. You'll get yourself killed and then what'll happen? Think of the town. Think of…Nester."

"Nester?" He looked as if she'd dumped a bucket of cold water over his head. "What does Nester have to do with me riding bulls?"

She spread her arms wide. "Everything, of course. If you get squashed he gets to be mayor. He'll be a terrible mayor, with all his talk of industry and tourism. He'll ruin Tranquility."

She perused the four-legged crew ready to stomp Gray and anyone else who got near. "You cannot ride a bull…for the sake of the town, I mean. Do something else at the rodeo if you want to partake in the festivities."

He put his fists on his hips. "Maybe I should bake a pie."

She held her hands out and cocked her head. "Well, there you go. I knew you'd come up with something else to do."

Gray exhaled a deep breath. "Nester won't get elected. The town will be safe. And everybody knows Ms. Rose bakes the best pies. I couldn't even win a ribbon."

He slid off his hat, a piece of duct tape pulling loose from the brim, and raked his hair. "I'll have one of my boys walk you back to The Smokehouse. It's late."

Sunny turned on her heels and strode away, one of Gray's cowhands at her side. She mumbled, "He's sincerely nuts."

The young hand smiled down at her. "It's a cowboy thing. Gray'll be okay."

But what if Gray wasn't okay? Not till this moment, when she realized how much danger he was in, did she consider just how much she cared…really and truly cared about him. She'd used every trick she could think of to get him to do the rodeo, and now she'd give anything to keep him away from it.

This was all her fault. If something happened to him, it would be her fault, as well. She couldn't live with that. She had to get Gray out of the rodeo and away from those blasted bulls. But how?

HIGH NOON at the OK Corral. Actually, it was high noon at The Smokehouse on the Fourth of July, but that didn't sound very dramatic, and what she had planned was pretty darn dramatic. Sunny adjusted her stance in front of the partly scorched bar. If her plan succeeded, Gray would not be a happy cowboy. Too bad. She had to save him, even if he didn't want to be saved. She'd gotten him into this. The place was empty. Everyone was down by the rodeo, waiting for the events to begin.

Events? Men riding big nasty animals that could stomp their heads flatter than a pancake was not an event. Closer to a death wish. And they paid to get a chance to do it.

She wiped sweat from her forehead. It had nothing to do with the ninety-degree temperature outside, since The Smokehouse's air conditioner worked fine. She'd stayed up all night practicing just how to keep Gray from bull riding. He'd be furious, but she could deal with furious. What she couldn't deal with was Gray hurt…or worse.

She looked at the animated clock on the wall, a cowboy riding a bull, hooves kicking as each second ticked by. *How appropriate.* Suddenly Gray burst through the door, all cowboy in a splashy red vest and chaps, ready to ride. A slice of bright sunlight followed him in, then vanished as the door closed. Her heart lodged in her throat. He was always handsome, but this was a different kind of handsome. This was rugged-male handsome, take-no-prisoners handsome, danger-ous handsome. Desire swamped her. Right now she'd much rather be swamped with courage.

"Sunny?" Gray blinked, trying to adjust his sight to the dim interior—just as she knew he would. "Are you here? Norm said you wanted to see me."

"I'm by the bar. Take off your hat." She licked her lips.

"I'm needed at the pens. The rodeo events are start-ing. And why do you want my hat off?"

"It's in the way."

"Of what?"

She watched him blink a few more times as he re-moved his hat and slid it onto a table. He walked slowly toward her, boots clicking on the hardwood floor, ac-companied by the ominous clank of metal spurs. Those spurs were for riding bulls. Resolve settled in her gut. She calculated he was about halfway to her now, next to a big wooden post supporting the beams overhead. She eyed the post and estimated the distance from Gray to her. Then took the rope she held behind her back, twirled the lasso and let it go to land it neatly over Gray.

"I did it."

"Okay, you can throw a rope. Was there anything else you needed me for, because—"

She yanked the lasso tight and ran for the wooden

post behind him, dragging Gray smack up against it before he knew what was happening. Then she ran around
the post, securing him to it.

"I'm saving your butt whether you want it saved or
not." He fought to get out of the lasso as she added,
"Learned this from the twins."

He struggled more as she circled the post, securing
his shoulders as he yelled, "What the hell are you
doing?"

"Don't curse at a lady. What kind of cowboy does
that?"

"One who's been saddled with a Reno lunatic."

She ran around again, pulling in his middle.

"I'm going to strangle you."

"I have amnesia. That wouldn't be nice." She left a
space in her roping for his manly attributes—didn't
want to hurt the attributes—then secured his knees.

"Nice? You're talking to me about nice?"

She tied a knot at his feet, then stood and faced him.

"I can't believe you're doing this."

Panting, she planted her hands on her hips, letting her
heartbeat settle in below five hundred. "Look, Nester
would make a terrible mayor. He's on a power trip. Dillon needs your help. I'm doing this for a lot of reasons."

He strained at the ropes. "Let me out of here! It's
my life. If I want to risk my neck I will." He shut his
eyes and pulled in a deep settling breath. "I won't get
hurt. These bulls aren't like Slider. They're not raised
for the rodeo. They're just bulls with good bloodlines
for propagating the herd. Pets. Nothing more."

"Pets! Ha! Who chased you across the pasture on the way to a wedding? That was not a pet. That was a mean-spirited son of a gun intent on bodily harm. All I need is an hour till the bull-riding event is over." She smiled sweetly. "Then I'll come get you." She patted his cheek.

He glared, then yelled, "Smitty? Smitty, where are you? Jean? Anybody here?"

"You put him and Jean up at the Corner Stone, remember? I appreciate that." She grinned.

"Norm? Art?" he yelled again.

"They're helping down at the pens. I was hoping I didn't have to do this, but you seem hell-bent on yelling. I can't have someone hear you."

She untied his neckerchief, feeling the angry heat from his body surround her. "Don't you even think about gagging me, Sunny Kelly." His eyebrows narrowed; he ground his teeth.

She went around the post behind him. "You'll thank me later for this."

"Thank you! *Woman*, if there's one thing you can count on me *not* doing it's thanking you. Stringing you up by your toenails has definite possibilities, a one-way ticket back to Reno would work, but thanking you is—"

She slid the bandanna across his mouth and he mumbled more ill-tempered plans for her future. She tied the bandanna behind his head, then stood in front of him and gave him her best surly look. She pointed at herself. "*Woman?* Who do you think you're calling *woman?*"

He mumbled something else and shook his head, looking a lot like an angry bull himself.

"What?" She slid off the bandanna.

"I going to hunt you down and—"

She slid the bandanna back across his mouth. "Think of this as a rescue mission."

His face reddened.

She tsked. "You're going to rupture something important if you don't calm down."

She stepped away from him and surveyed her handiwork. "Told you I was going to lasso rowdy cowboys. Thanks for the lesson."

He said something that didn't sound pleasant and his eyes went bloodshot.

"Try to chill. And don't you dare hurt my bar by pulling and yanking things. I have to help Elizabeth set up the cotton-candy booth, then I'll be back." She was halfway toward the door when she turned, retraced her steps and slipped the gag from his mouth.

He snarled, "Finally came to your senses, huh?"

"Came for something else." She wrapped her arms around his neck and kissed him hard on the mouth, tasting his anger, his frustration and his maleness. She really liked the maleness part. Then she replaced the gag and ran out the door like the devil himself was after her.

Chapter Eight

"I'm going to strangle Sunny Kelly within an inch of her life," Gray said to Doc as he unwound the rope. "Sure glad you showed up when you did."

"Ms. Rose forgot her sweater last night and I stopped by to pick it up. Seems everybody but us is at the rodeo."

"I think that's what Sunny counted on. Where did she get this dang-fool obsession about me not riding bulls?" Gray snatched his hat from the table, remembering how sweetly she'd asked him to remove it so she could get her damn lasso around his head.

"Come on." He took Doc's arm. "I've got a date with Slingshot and you've got to put a blue ribbon on Ms. Rose's apple pie before Junior makes his move. I think he's getting ready to pop the question and—"

"There is no pie."

Gray stopped on the front porch and gave Doc a sympathetic look. "Dang, Ms. Rose must be in a real snit to not even enter the contest. I'm sorry about... Maybe we can think of something to—"

"We ate it."

Gray did a double take.

"For breakfast." He realized Doc had on new glasses and his toupee was gone. His hair was neatly combed—not even a combover. His clothes were pressed and he was smiling like a kid at Christmas with a new toy. "After dancing at the wedding, I suppose we both had a few beers too many and…" Doc's gray eyes sparkled. "Rosie and beer…" Red crawled up his neck. "My stars. That woman sure can…dance."

Doc pointed down the street. "You better get a move on. And don't you go being too hard on Sunny when you find her. She wouldn't have tied you up like a Thanksgiving turkey if she didn't care about you."

Gray lowered his eyelids and stared at Doc. "She tied me up because she's worried Nester will take over Tranquility if something happens to me."

Doc laughed till he hiccuped. "If you're believing that cockamamy story, Gray McBride, you got cow pies for brains." He winked and took off down the street whistling a dance tune, with Ms. Rose's white sweater draped over his arm. Gray headed in the other direction at a dead run.

Well, hell. Doc had had apple pie for breakfast with Ms. Rose, and he'd had a Pop-Tart alone, standing over the kitchen sink, drinking milk from the carton. And what did Doc mean that Gray had cow pies for brains? Sunny said she was worried about Nester and the town. Those were her exact words.

Nope, Doc was wrong. He and Sunny shared a physical attraction—one hell of a *strong* physical attraction—sprinkled with bouts of mutual admiration. Nothing more. She'd tied him up because of the election. *Everything they did was for the blasted election.* Not that he had anyone to blame except himself…and his hardheaded brother.

Gray tore past the flags and bunting and ribbons on Oak Street, running toward the sound of cheering crowds, rodeo announcements and the familiar scents of hay, horses, dirt and cattle.

He could tell from the announcements that calf roping was in full swing and he knew bull riding came next. Gray turned for the rodeo corral but spotted Sunny cutting across Main, walking toward the cattle pens.

He crossed the street and came up behind her, careful to keep his spurs and boots as quiet as possible, aiming to surprise her as she'd surprised him. He dropped his hand on her shoulder. "Having a busy Fourth of July, are we?"

Just seeing the startled, then confused, then exasperated look on her face, made it worth having gotten tied up. She planted her hands on her hips. "How tall are you?"

"Uh, six-one. Why?"

"Walnut or mahogany?"

"What do you mean, walnut or mahogany? What kind of dumb question is that?"

"Just pick one."

"Mahogany."

"I'll pass the information on to the undertaker when they scrape up your pitiful hide with a spatula after that bull tromps you flat. 'Course, the coffin will only have to be two inches thick, so it shouldn't be too expensive."

"Cute, very cute." And she was, *dammit*, with her red peasant blouse catching the breeze and her golden hair framing her lovely face. He listened to the announcement about the bull-riding events. "We'll finish this when I get back." He took a few steps, then turned. "You going to watch me ride or what?"

His gaze fused with hers and there was something in her eyes, something he hadn't noticed before. Concern? Fear? What?

He heard the announcement for the bull riding again.

"Try not to bleed all over Main Street. It'll stain. Give Tranquility a bad reputation. Though Nester's going to do that all by himself once he gets elected mayor, because you'll be pushing up daisies."

"I'll take that as a *no*." He started for the rodeo corral, then heard her say, "Just be safe, Gray McBride."

He stopped, spun around and stared at her while his name was announced as the next rider. What did she just say? Be safe? No mention of Nester or the election or needing Gray to take care of the town. And she'd had a sincere look in her eyes he'd never seen before.

Ah, hell. This was not the time or place to figure out Sunny Kelly. An unfocused bull rider was a dead-as-a-doornail bull rider.

He ran to the shoot. The announcer blabbed on about Slingshot's attributes as one mean son-of-a-gun bull and Gray's accomplishments as one fine bull rider. Gray adjusted his chaps and settled on the back of the beast. The bull snorted and stomped his hooves as Gray took the bull rope. He thought of Sunny's words, her eyes staring at him, filled with...

Concentrate, he ordered himself. *Bear down. Stay over your hand. Forget about Sunny Kelly.*

The buzzer sounded, the gate flew open, Slingshot snarled and bucked forward and Gray pictured golden hair and soft full lips. Slingshot snorted and reared and Gray thought of long legs and an exciting laugh. Slingshot pitched and twisted and Gray remembered smooth skin and green eyes filled with genuine concern and caring. Then he felt himself fly ass-over-appetite into the air and land butt first in the dirt, jarring every bone in his body.

He scrambled to safety over the fence as Slingshot did the bull version of a victory dance and the announcer ragged Gray for a pathetic ride. As Gray left the ring, Smitty handed Gray his hat. "What happened out there, cowboy?"

"Where's Sunny?"

"Last time I saw her she was at the bull pen, looking sick as all get out. Said there was no way she'd watch you ride some bull and break your dang-fool neck. Why?"

Gray slapped Smitty on the back. "I'll fill you in later." *She cared*...really cared about *him*. Not just the town or winning the election, but him. Imagine that.

But how did he feel about her? The same way? He never thought about caring…really caring in an intimate way…about Sunny. He rounded the corner of the hardware store and saw her tearing through the bull pen, one of the twins hanging on to her for all he was worth, a lasso dangling from his little hand and Bone Crusher charging after them like a runaway freight train.

Holy hell! Gray's heart stopped. Terror shot through him. Three other cowboys realized the gravity of the situation at the same time he did and jumped into the ring to divert Bone Crusher. Except the bull had one thing on his mind right now—Sunny Kelly with a three-year-old cradled in her arms.

SUNNY'S LUNGS BURNED as she ran as fast as she could. Why had little Ben…or was this Joey…tried to lasso a bull? Couldn't he lasso a chicken?

"Sunny."

She looked over and saw Gray running next to her. Where'd he come from? He snatched Ben/Joey from her. Out of the corner of her eye she saw other cowboys jumping around and yelling, trying to get Bone Crusher's attention. But this bull was a one-girl guy. An admirable attribute in a male…usually.

He lowered his head, charging faster. Hay bales and fence loomed. Safety, home free…if she could jump six feet straight up and over the barricade. *Great!*

Bone Crusher's hot, wet, snotty breath fell across her back in short fierce snorts. *Yuck.* Desperate now, she closed her eyes and dived for the bales. She was nowhere near the six feet needed to clear them but got instantly hauled over by helping hands. She landed headfirst into the dirt, then the fence shuddered as Bone Crusher forgot to apply brakes and collided with it, scaring the bejeebers out of her...*like she had any bejeebers left!*

She felt Gray's hands on her, turning her over. She'd know his touch anywhere. "Sunny, open your eyes. Say something."

"Think I'll be a vegetarian." It took her a second to find some more breath. "How's Ben? Or was it Joey? Why are there two of you? One's enough."

"Ben's fine. Thought it was great fun and wants to do it again tomorrow. What hurts? Anything broken?"

His hands felt her legs, then worked their way up her thighs to her hips and waist and ribs. Gray may not have intended to turn her on but he did, and with an audience present. She sat up. "I'm okay." She forced a grin and held up her hands in triumph. "I'm fine. Wonderful."

She tried to stand, but Gray pushed her down. "Just sit tight. I'm getting Doc."

She shoved Gray's hands away and scrambled up, stumbling twice. "No need for that. I'm going to The Smokehouse. Got things to do for tonight." She held on to the pen for support and grinned at the cowboys who'd gathered around. "Thanks for hauling me over the fence. Stop in tonight at the saloon—your drinks are on the house."

The cowboys left, bragging about who'd drink who under the table. "Dammit, Sunny. You…you scared the hell out of me."

"Yeah, well, seeing one of the twins in with that bull didn't do me any good, either."

"I wasn't just talking about Ben."

Now what? *Oh, Gray, I care about you, too* was not the thing to say. "Where're Elizabeth and Dillon?"

"Recovering from heart failure." He pulled in a deep breath. "I'll get Norm to take you home. I think people are getting suspicious about us being together."

"Your ride went well. Your head's still attached to your neck."

He looked serious. "I want to see you."

She held her hands wide. "Ta-da. Here I am."

He didn't appear amused. "Meet me on The Smoke-house roof. Tonight."

"Isn't that a little extreme?"

"Hell, it's the only place I can think of where we won't be interrupted, stared at or overheard. Everyone else will be at the fireworks."

Gray left, and she tried to focus, hoping things stood still. She spotted Norm coming around the corner, wagging his head as he approached. "Heard you had a race with a bull and won by a nose, or was it a snort? You got to remember four legs are twice as fast as two."

"Yeah, but I won." She cocked her head and rolled her shoulders, trying to realign all the little bones in her back and neck. "I think I won." He fell into step beside her and they moseyed toward the saloon. *Mosey* was her top speed at the moment.

Norm rubbed his hands together. "Uh, I got a favor to ask. An old friend got trampled up pretty bad last year as a rodeo clown and he's having a devil of a time finding a job. I don't want you to think of him as a charity case—he's willing to work and all—but—"

"We can find something. Auntie would have wanted it that way."

Norm grinned. "I really appreciate it. He plays the guitar and sings a little."

This time Sunny grinned. "Well, heck. Why didn't you say so? Tell your friend he's just want we need at The Smokehouse. Maybe he knows songs about hard-headed cowboys who ride bulls that could trample them flatter than a dollar bill. He could sing them to Gray."

Not that he'd ever hear the songs. After tonight, the rodeo was over. And there'd be no reason for them to be together. He'd get busy with the campaign and being mayor and helping at the Lazy K and forget about her. She had the saloon. Or maybe she'd go back to Reno. Someday she had to go back and figure out what was going on there…unless someone from there came looking for her. Whichever happened, she had to forget Gray McBride.

Her logic made perfect sense until that night, when she saw Gray from her perch on top of the roof. A jolt of excitement skittered up her spine the way it always did when she spotted him. *Forget Gray?* No matter how many times she got amnesia, she'd never forget him. But she couldn't have him. His family got first dibs.

"Hey," she called down to the deserted street…deserted except for Gray. He glanced up and she waved. "We can watch the fireworks. The ladder's still around back from when we put a new roof on the place."

Gray disappeared, and a minute later she heard his footsteps on the roof. He sat down beside her on a blanket she'd spread out, and looked around at the streetlights below. "Kind of like watching a play…but the actors aren't onstage yet."

She leaned back on her elbows, gazing at the starry canopy above. A shooting star cut across the sky. Being with Gray was like that star, an incredibly fast and memorable trip to nowhere. "So cowboy, how big a success was your rodeo?"

"*Our* rodeo." Gray smiled her way. "Along with the money set aside to buy The Smokehouse, we might have made enough to build a smaller firehouse and probably get me elected mayor in the bargain."

"The town council isn't interested in buying the saloon and making it part of the firehouse now?"

"That's still the cheapest way to go, but The Smokehouse brings a lot of people and their money to town. The council likes that a lot." He faced her. "Why didn't you want me to ride the bulls this afternoon?"

Uh-oh. This was not something she wanted to get into. Mostly because, like the shooting star, her fretting over his bull riding went nowhere. "I simply couldn't. Nester's a dweeb. End of story."

Gray's eyes darkened. "I don't believe you."

"Trust me, Gray. Nester is really a dweeb. He's willing to sacrifice the long-term good of the town for immediate short-term goals that appeal to some people who can't see any farther than the end of their nose and—"

"This has nothing to do with Nester. It's between you and me. Smitty said that while I was riding Slingshot you were at the bull pen, losing your lunch."

Did anyone in this town ever mind their own business? "Good grief, it was ninety. I'd just tied up a cowboy with a bad attitude. My nerves were frazzled."

A strand of hair fell over his forehead. "You kissed me, hard. You weren't frazzled. You were sexy and flirty and hot…and it had nothing to do with summer heat." He stroked her cheek and his face turned serious. "I could have lost you today."

Her heart swelled. She didn't want it to. She didn't want any reaction to Gray at all. She didn't want Gray to care about her and her to care about him, because what could they do about it? Lust was a lot easier to deal with.

He slowly brought his face to hers. Their lips were nearly touching. "I always want you. And not just in my bed. I want you in my life." He sighed, his breath falling across her mouth. "But I know that can't happen."

"It could happen right now."

"I want more."

She framed his face with her hands. "Gray, all we've

ever had is *right now*." She kissed him and bliss mixed with ecstasy as he took her in his arms and kissed her back. His hands slid under her blouse and she shivered with wanting him, her breasts full and heavy in anticipation of his touch. She wrapped her arms around his broad, very male shoulders as his tongue explored her mouth.

She fumbled with the buttons on his shirt, needing to feel the soft curls and hard muscles of his chest. She wanted to explore every inch of the terrific cowboy build that she'd ogled since she'd woken up in the clinic. She ran her hands over him, loving the feel of his nipples against her palm. Then she parted his shirt and planted a row of soft kisses where her hands had been.

His BREATH CAUGHT. Passion roared, drowning out all thoughts of the election and other things standing in their way of being together. He leaned her back onto the blanket and unbuttoned her blouse, exposing her delectable skin inch by inch. "I can never get enough of you."

He eased his fingers under her bra, feeling the silky smoothness of her breasts, then pushed it up, to reveal pink nipples.

Her eyes danced as he unsnapped her shorts and fireworks exploded overhead, lighting the sky with red, white and blue. She kicked off her sandals, one skidding down the roof, toppling to the ground.

More fireworks showered the world in white and

blue glitter as she undid the button on his jeans. She took his erection into her warm, soft hands and he thought he'd vaporize right into the sky with the fireworks.

He looked into her eyes, seeing the parade of lights reflected there. "You're gorgeous and exciting and unforgettable."

She stroked him again, nearly taking him to the breaking point, then reached into his back pocket and pulled out his wallet. "Driver's license, two credit cards, receipt for extrahot buffalo wings from Durango's." She chuckled. "Those things will kill you."

He gritted his teeth. "You're the one doing that. A man's only got so much control." He pulled out a condom.

She gazed at him with dreamy eyes and slowly spread her thighs, welcoming him into her body. She wrapped her legs around his middle, encouraging him...not that he needed it. Then she arched her hips and he thrust inside her, making her a part of him, knowing she wanted that, too. Her eyes clouded, her breath strained as she breathed his name into the night, and they climaxed together, two mismatched people in the most unlikely place.

He held her tight, committing to memory the feel of her under him, the heat of her smooth skin next to his, their bodies damp with perspiration and lovemaking, their limbs wound together tight. His head sagged onto her shoulder and he inhaled the wonderful exciting scent so uniquely Sunny.

She held him as if not ready for him to leave, as if she'd never be ready for him to leave. "If I'd ever made love like this before I would have remembered. No amnesia, no anything, could make me forget something this wonderful." She kissed his cheek, then whispered in his ear, "I'll always remember tonight, Gray. I'll always remember you and the time we've spent together."

His heart squeezed tight. "Damn the election. Damn the Lazy K. Damn everything that's in the way of us."

His eyes held hers for several heartbeats; he did not want to let this moment pass. They'd never talked about just the two of them before. Maybe because something else always got in the way. "Are you sorry we made love?"

She shook her head. "Dillon needs you more than ever. Did you know he was talking business on his cell phone when Ben went into that bull pen? Dillon's stretched too thin, and when the new baby comes…"

He gently put his fingertips to her sweet lips. "Let's not talk about all that. Let's talk about how you are so incredibly lovely in the moonlight…and the sunlight…any light at all."

Her eyes went smoky and he grew hard, wanting her all over again. He'd always be ready to make love to her, anytime, anywhere.

"The fireworks are over. People will be heading back. Norm and Art will open up The Smokehouse for late-night customers. If we get caught together up here it won't do your reputation one bit of good and all your hard work on the rodeo will be for nothing."

He slammed his hand against the roof. "I hate sneaking around and making love to you on rooftops and pool tables and not telling the world we're together and I want us to stay that way."

"We're nothing, Gray."

Her words stung like a million bees, but he couldn't think of a suitable reply because she was right. He rolled off her and handed her the panties and shorts. "I liked it a lot more when I was taking these off you."

He stole one final look at the woman he cared for more than any woman he'd ever met. He wasn't the kind of man who slipped in and out of the shadows like some lowlife to get what he wanted. When he knew what he wanted, he went after it, no holds barred.

But this time he couldn't. He owed Dillon; he owed his family. They needed him and he had to win this election. He'd come too far to turn back now. "I don't want it to be over between us, Sunny."

"For right now it is. Elizabeth just drove up and parked across the street. And when she comes across my sandal lying on the ground she'll look up and she won't just see the moon and the stars."

He heard doors open and shut and a familiar child's voice say, "Mommy, I'm sleepy."

What the heck? Gray peered over the front of the saloon. "She has the twins."

Sunny dressed…except for her sandals. "Why is she here at this hour with the boys? Where do you suppose Dillon is? He's not with her."

Gray ran his hand across the back of his neck. "He

has an early meeting in Dallas tomorrow. He's probably driving out tonight."

Elizabeth stopped the stroller in front of The Smokehouse and bent down. She retrieved the sandal, glanced around, then craned her neck. "Sunny? Gray? Hope I'm not interrupting anything. Well, actually, I hope I am…but we can talk about that later. If Sunny doesn't mind, the kids and I are moving in. She seems to have room for everyone who needs it, and right now the kids and I need a place to stay until I get something more permanent. I'm leaving Dillon…not that he'll even know I'm gone. *I've had it.*"

Chapter Nine

Sunny nearly slid off the roof as she stared down at Elizabeth. "You're leav—"

She swallowed the rest of her words. Folks straggling back from the fireworks shouldn't hear McBride family details shouted from the rooftop…though they'd hear soon enough via the Tranquility back-fence report. CNN had nothing on the town gossips. "Don't move. I'll be down in a minute to help you with the kids."

But Art beat her to it. He crossed the street and hoisted the stroller—twins and all—onto the front porch of the saloon. Nothing like a strong cowboy to get the job done. Sunny turned for the ladder and bumped flat into Gray. He wasn't moving; his mouth gaped; his eyes were unfocused. Even strong sexy cowboys felt powerless sometimes. She grabbed his shoulders. "Take a deep breath. We'll get this little problem between Elizabeth and Dillon worked out. It's going to be okay." *I hope!*

"Dillon can't lose Elizabeth and the kids. What the hell did my thickheaded brother do now?"

"Not much, and I'm guessing that's the whole trouble." She followed Gray down the ladder. Just once she'd like to make love with him in a bed. They entered the saloon through the back door. Joey and Ben sat sleepy-eyed and docile in the stroller till they spotted Gray. As if spring-mounted, they jumped out and made a beeline for him, chanting, "Uncle Gray, Uncle Gray. Piggyback ride. Piggyback ride."

He bent down to the giggling, squirming boys. They climbed on, back and chest, holding tight with legs and arms. The baby-opossum approach. Gray laughed. "Let's go upstairs and have a sleepover at Sunny's. She has a big double bed you and your mom can share. In the morning you can sit at the bar and Art will make you silver-dollar pancakes."

Elizabeth flashed Gray a tired smile of thanks as he snatched the duffels and headed for the steps, the boys still clinging, Six yapping and prancing as if tickled to the tip of his windshield-wiper tail to see the twins again. Art turned for the little kitchen. "I'll get some herbal tea and the almond cookies that Norm made fresh this morning."

Sunny pushed the stroller to one side, then ushered Elizabeth to a table and sat across from her as Maxine and Hal, Connie and Dixon, Bea and her sister and other familiar patrons meandered into the saloon. Gus and Tommy Lee and a group of cowboys followed. Some went to the bar and others found tables and punched up the jukebox. She gave a welcoming wave to Norm's friend, Clyde, as he tied on a bar apron and started taking orders. Art sauntered in with a cute red-head at his side and started loading long necks onto a tray. Without these guys—and some good advice from *Reader's Digest*—there'd be no Smokehouse. She leaned over the table toward Elizabeth and asked in a whisper, "Okay. Give. What the heck happened to make you walk out on your husband?"

Elizabeth sat back in the chair, her fingers tapping in time to the music, and said loud enough for anyone near to hear, "I have no husband. I married a paycheck. Dillon's never around. I have to call his assistant to find out where he is. Last week he read the boys a good-night story over the phone. It was a financial report with income and revenue as the good guys, loss and deficit the bad guys and tax abatement the fairy god-mother. What kind of father is that?"

"Amen," agreed Maxine. She raised her beer in salute to Elizabeth. "The men around here have to stay home nights once in a while and that includes Dillon." She nudged her husband. "And you. I've been telling you that same thing for years."

Elizabeth thanked Clyde for the tea. "Maybe moving out will get Dillon's attention. I don't know how else to make him listen to me other than tying him up."

Sunny huffed, "Trust me, it's been done and that doesn't work, either."

Elizabeth gave her a questioning look as Connie turned her attention to the conversation, nodding in sympathy, which sent her red, white and blue rhinestone earrings dancing. "Men think they can drop in and pleasure the missus once in a while, then take off and do their thing. That's what they've been doing forever in this town. Like it's some kind of tradition. I'm starting to think this is one bad tradition. Actually, I've been thinking that for some time now, and Elizabeth here just proves my point."

"I agree," chimed in Heather, Bea's sister. She raised her beer in agreement. "Takes two to make the kids and two to raise them, but men in Tranquility don't seem to get that."

"Now just hold on a minute," chimed in her boyfriend. He pushed his black Stetson to the back of his head, a slow sexy smile tripping across his face. "Dillon's a fine man and damn good provider. What's so hard to understand about that? He's got to go off and be the breadwinner. He can't be hanging around the house all the time."

Bea and her sister pursed their lips in disapproval. "Now you tell me why it has to be Dillon going off? Why not Elizabeth? She's a fine financial attorney. And even if the women want to stay home, they need help with the kids and a night out once in a while. The guys sure take their nights out."

Gus gulped his beer. "Seems to me that raising the kids is Elizabeth's work."

"And siring them is Dillon's?" retorted the cute redhead who'd come in with Norm.

Gus shrugged. "Well, now that you mention it."

His wife playfully punched his arm, though the sudden glint in her eyes suggested she'd like to omit the playful part. "So Dillon should just come around to sow his…oats and then leave?"

"And what's this about raising the kids being Elizabeth's work?" added Maxine.

Tommy Lee added, "Hell, that's sure the way I see it. That's the way my daddy did it and his daddy."

His wife took the beer from his hand and set it back on the table hard. Her eyes beaded. "With an attitude like that you'll be sleeping on the couch tonight and maybe some other nights until you change your tune. Tell your daddy about that. 'Bout time you helped more around the house and with the kids. Elizabeth's predicament has made me see the light." She surveyed the room. "Think it's made all of us see it. She just up and did something about it. If it wasn't that our eldest could finally do a little baby-sitting, I wouldn't be here tonight, but you sure would."

She tipped her chin. "Just for your information, I'm thinking about going back to nursing school. So put that in your pipe and smoke it."

"And you," chimed in Heather to her boyfriend, "can forget about any September wedding till you readjust your thinking about who's having kids and who's raising them and just where the hell you'll be during all this."

Maxine faced Hal. "And why do I always cook dinner, hmm? Can't you cook it once in a while? Or is that woman's work, too? I know how to change a tire on a car. Seems to me you should be able to cook. 'Bout time you read a cookbook instead of *Rodeo Weekly*."

He held up his hands in self-defense. "Now just a minute, I didn't say cooking was women's work."

Her eyes narrowed to thin slits. "Yeah, but you were thinking it." She fluffed her graying bob. "I'm going on strike. Fact is, I'm opening a beauty parlor…been thinking about it for some time. And now's the time. Redo the garage where you park that hunk-of-junk truck of yours. I'll do manicure and pedicures and everything. Always wanted to own a beauty parlor. Used to have Beauty Parlor Barbie when I was a girl. *You* can cook your own darn dinner."

Maxine stood. "I'm needing a little space right now, a little *woman* space to think about all this." She snatched up Elizabeth by the arm. "And it's all thanks to Elizabeth for getting the ball rolling and walking out on Dillon. And to Sunny, of course, for redoing The Smokehouse so womenfolk feel welcome. Heck, that's what got us here and talking tonight. 'Bout time women in Tranquility were appreciated for who they really are."

Maxine nodded, agreeing with her own words. "If anyone wants to join us I'll be making a batch of margaritas…and a pot of peppermint tea…on the back porch over at my place, in honor of Tranquility's women. There's more to family life than men sitting their butts at the table, scarfing dinner and keeping the sheets tangled." She tossed her head again and headed for the door, followed by a parade of other discontent women.

Sunny called to Elizabeth, "I'll watch the boys. Don't worry about a thing."

The men stared slack-jawed and openmouthed as the females paraded out the door, backbones straight, backsides doing a take-that sashay that only women on a mission can do.

Tommy Lee huffed, "What the hell just happened?" His eyebrows drew together. "This is all Dillon McBride's fault." He pointed to Elizabeth as she left. "If he hadn't gone off she wouldn't be here and I wouldn't be sleeping on the couch tonight."

"And I wouldn't be without dinner," added Hal as he patted his rounded belly. "I can't cook. Don't even know how to use that dang-fool microwave contraption." He scratched his head. "How'd this get from Dillon and Elizabeth to all of us?"

Gray strode into the bar and gazed around. "What's going on this time?"

Tommy Lee scowled. "Where in the Sam Hill is that brother of yours?"

Gray shifted his eyes right, then left, taking in the mood, as if not sure how to reply. "Why?"

"Because he's got this town in a fine mess."

"He's not even here. How could he do that?"

"You get ahold of him and tell him to get his wife back to the Lazy K where she belongs—"

"Where *she* belongs!" Sunny stood, hands on hips.

Three men at the end of the bar nodded. The women with them jutted their chins, slid from their stools and made for the door with the others.

Gus walked over to Gray and put his hands firmly on Gray's shoulders, looking him dead in the eye. "For

God's sake, boy, find Dillon and get him back here. As long as Elizabeth's in town, our wives and girlfriends will keep thinking how we're never around to lend a hand. I'll miss my poker night and bowling night and weekly cattlemen's meetings."

The men grumbled their agreement and hunched over their beers as if guarding the last thing on earth they controlled. Gray approached the table with Sunny. "What did you do?"

"Are the kids okay? And all I did was open The Smokehouse." She rolled her shoulders. "The women did the rest...and it's about time."

"Six is there. I left the doors open so we can hear if the boys call, but I think they're zonked." He surveyed the sullen male population, then sat down across from Sunny. "I'll check in a few minutes to make sure. I'm betting Dillon doesn't even know Elizabeth's gone. There wasn't a mushroom cloud from the fallout over the ranch."

"There will be. The only thing that's going to fix any of this is for you to win the election and have Dillon turn over ranch responsibility to you so he can spend more time with Elizabeth. Maybe the men around here will take the hint and do the same, making their wives happy. Things will get back to normal."

Gray folded his arms and studied her with dark brown eyes that made her stomach turn flips. "With a new female twist?"

"Elizabeth probably didn't bargain for all this notoriety. Funny how things just snowball."

He looked at the men. "They're not laughing." He stroked his chin. "How in the hell did I go from the simple idea of expanding the firehouse to getting the men and women of Tranquility back together?"

She patted his arm, loving the feel of him against her fingertips. Wishing she could feel him all over. "Benjamin Franklin called it politics."

"I'll track down Dillon tomorrow." Gray sat back in the chair and said to the guys, "This place looks like a damn funeral parlor."

Gus huffed, "Bet the women aren't having a funeral. Bet they're kicking up their heels and making plans... none that will do us one damn bit of good. I feel like a cow at branding time."

"Yeah," added Dixon. "And I'm here to tell you it's much better being the bull at breeding time. Don't know if things are ever going to be the same around Tranquility. Our women got ideas of their own now. Dang. How'd that happen? His shoulders sagged. "And I just bought a new bowling ball. Bet their new ideas aren't going to be good for my bowling ball."

Sunny tapped her finger to her lips. "I could open The Smokehouse for luncheons."

Every eye turned to her. "Serve salad and quiche."

Gray sat straight in his chair. *"This is a damn cowboy bar. No quiche."*

"It's not a cowboy bar at lunch. It's closed at lunch. I could put a few tables out back. Make a garden. Flowers on the tables."

Hal slid off his bar stool, Gus dropped his beer,

Tommy Lee folded his arms on the table and buried his head. Sunny stood. "Good grief. It's just lunch. No flower aroma will desecrate the sacred odor of stale beer and cigarettes." She faced Gray. "I'll go upstairs and check on the boys."

Gray ordered a round of beers on him. Every guy in the place needed it. He caught up with Sunny as she started for the steps. "I'll keep an eye on the place tonight. And, just for the record, I like the independent-women idea." A slow easy grin settled on his lips. "Especially women who run saloons. They're sexy and fun and exciting. My kind of gal."

"And completely off-limits."

"At one time they weren't, but they are now. And it's too damn bad."

She climbed the stairs, opened the door to her apartment and crept toward the bedroom. Babies sleeping. Could anything be more peaceful? Knowing Elizabeth, she wouldn't be gone long. Tonight she'd share the bed with the boys and maybe get some rest. It would help her prepare for tomorrow…when Dillon McBride showed up and all hell broke loose.

GRAY SAT in his new truck and yawned. He checked his watch—3:00 a.m. All quiet. After the Fourth of July celebration and the Tranquility Women's Independence Day, the whole town was dead asleep…though most of the male population was doing their sleeping on the couch. Right now he'd settle for a couch, especially with Sunny next to him…or under him. Dang, he wanted her.

When *didn't* he want her? Every time she came into a room or he saw her across the street his heart skipped a beat. Being with her brightened his day to no end. More and more he wanted to hear her voice, her laughter; see her happy face and golden hair; hear about the latest cowboy she'd taken on and added to The Smokehouse payroll. But—

Something moved in the shadows at the far end of The Smokehouse. Gray snapped alert, straightening, the leather seat crinkling softly under the shift of weight. He held his breath and peered at the same place to make sure his eyes weren't playing tricks. It moved again…and Elizabeth, the kids and Sunny were upstairs.

Noiselessly he slid from the truck, not clicking the door shut, keeping to the bushes and trees. He slinked his way across the street, then to the side of The Smokehouse. As he turned the corner a man in a baseball cap spied him, and their eyes locked for an instant. The man clambered up the front steps, across the porch and dropped something at the front door. Gray readied to give chase, then felt another person move behind him. He spun around to snatch him by the arm…except it was a *her*. Sunny yelped.

"*Dang, girl*. What the hell are you doing here?"

"I live here, and that guy's getting away." She ran around Gray, up the front steps and across the porch after the intruder, who catapulted himself over the railing to the ground below. Gray ran after her, snagging her back to keep her from doing the same thing.

"Let me go." She tried to jerk free, furious at him.

"Elizabeth and the boys are upstairs. We have to stay here and make sure The Smokehouse is safe. Let him go, Sunny. We'll lose him in the dark." *And he was not about to have her running after some bad guy in the dead of night.*

She panted and nodded, leaning against the railing to catch her breath. "You're right. Elizabeth and the twins are more important."

And you. Definitely you, he thought as he studied her in the moonlight. Sunny in danger made his insides cold with fear. But he couldn't use that as an excuse not to follow the intruder, because Sunny wouldn't buy into it for a second. She was fearless, taking on jobs that seemed impossible. "What were you doing up at this hour anyway?"

"Couldn't sleep. There's something going on and it's not a good thing. I was worried."

Gray walked back to the front door and picked up what the intruder had dropped. "It's a toy truck. A cement truck."

Sunny drew up beside him as he continued, "What the hell did you have going on with cement when you were in Reno?" His eyes held hers. "I watch The Sopranos. Things cement are not good omens."

She pulled a rolled-up piece of paper from the back end of the truck and read: "'Don't Forget.'" She sighed. "Easy for him to say…whoever *him* is…but I can't remember one darn thing about cement."

Gray turned the truck over, examining it from every

angle. Then he turned his attention back to Sunny. Big blue T-shirt, bare feet, rumpled golden bed hair, green eyes smudged with sleep. The sight of her made all his defenses to resist her crumple into a meaningless heap. He ached to take her in his arms and hold her, make love to her, kiss every inch of her wonderful body all night long. Instead, he handed her back the truck and said, "You don't know anything about this?"

She crossed one bare foot over the other, her T-shirt sliding gently over the peaks of her lovely nipples, making him hard as stone. *Damnation.*

"Well, there was this guy in the alley a few days ago with terrible beer breath, who did happen to mention I should pay him."

Gray's uncomfortable physical condition was suddenly the least of his problems. "Guy? What guy? Who this time? Crimany, Sunny! What have you gotten into?"

She gave him a narrow-eyed look. "Don't crimany me. This isn't my fault. You think I enjoy being dragged into dark alleys and getting called girlie-girl? He actually called me that." She huffed and stood tall, giving him a hint of her bare body underneath. "Just who does he think he is calling me girlie-girl? I have a name. If he's going to threaten me he can darn well call me by my name."

"Why didn't you tell me this before now? You could have been hurt…or worse."

"Probably not."

"You think you're invincible?"

"No, I think I'm the meal ticket." She ran her hand through her sexy-as-hell sleep-tousled hair. His forgotten condition returned with a vengeance.

"This guy wants me to pay up. Actually, it's his boss who wants the money. I can't very well do that if I'm pushing up daisies. So I'm safe."

"Until he or his boss gets tired of warning and decides to do something drastic so you take them seriously." Desire mixed with concern. He wanted to make love to her *and* lock her in a room somewhere to keep her safe. Both at the same time had definite appeal...except the whole darn town would know by dawn and he could kiss his election goodbye. *"Damnation."*

"Before you get a first-class tirade going, let's check out the rest of the saloon to make sure this toy is all he left."

"You go inside and wait and *I'll*—"

"Yeah, yeah, yeah." She waved in the air and made for the side of the house. "How about *you* go inside," she said over her shoulder. "This is my bar, my fight. My cement problem."

He followed, mumbling every swearword he could think of and making up a few new ones along the way. He was entitled. She was driving him crazy and there wasn't one damn thing he could do about it.

They crept from the side to the back to the other side. They stayed in the shadows, watching for anything else out of the ordinary, though when it came to The Smokehouse, what was ordinary? "Whoever it was seemed only intent on leaving you the truck."

Gray pushed back his hat and held up the truck to examine it. "Does it trigger anything at all?"

She leaned against the saloon and massaged her forehead. "I do remember something about cement. Money's involved, but I don't know how much or who or why. One thing's for sure, though—I don't get good vibes from this truck…in fact, I feel like I'm going to end up in one if I don't figure this all out soon."

"You need to tell Leroy."

"The Smokehouse is on a roll and I'm not doing anything to interfere with that. I'm not the only one with a future in the place. Norm, Art, Smitty, Jean and now Clyde have their futures here, as well. I can't put all that at risk over some cement."

"A Reno showgirl with a heart of gold."

Pink crept into her cheeks; he could tell even in the dim light. She studied the dirt by her bare feet. "It's a financial decision. Ground-floor initiative and co-determination practices by all workers ensure bottom-line net profit."

He tipped her chin, bringing her face to his, moonlight dancing in her eyes. He smoothed the curls from her forehead and kissed where the curls had been. "I think that's double talk for being an old softy." He stepped closer. "You are the most beautiful woman I've ever laid eyes on. Inside and out. I try like hell to get over you, and nothing, not one damn thing, works. Not speeches I give myself about how you're the wrong girl for me, or feelings of obligation for how much I need to help the family." He kissed her, savoring her taste, her warmth, her incredible sensuality that made him forget everything but being with her.

"I can't get you out of my system." He kissed her again, relishing the feel of her tongue with his, her body in his arms. Stolen time. Time they shouldn't be together. Memorable, earth-shattering, incredible time. Her nipples hardened against his chest; her breathing came hot and fast across his face. Her fingers stopped at his belt and she gazed into his eyes. "I want you."

Her eyes blazed for him as fire blasted through him. He helped with the zipper and located protection. She slid off her panties and he backed her to the wooden wall of The Smokehouse, cupped her derriere as her legs twined around his middle, and he thrust himself inside her—hard, possessive, desperate. She was his, all his…just for now, just for a moment. Just one more time. He kissed her, swallowing her gasp as the world exploded around him, and they climaxed in a wondrous world created for them alone.

THE NEXT DAY Sunny watched through the front window of The Smokehouse as Gray jogged up the steps. Behind him the evening sun peeked through the last rain clouds, transforming Tranquility into one big sauna. All day she'd looked out that window, not because rain fascinated her, but because she hoped to see Gray. She wanted to be with him but couldn't, so she'd settle for a look. That wouldn't put his election at risk. Being at The Smokehouse wasn't unusual, since nearly every man in Tranquility was having dinner here and Gray's brother was the reason.

Gray walked between men at the bar munching Dagwoods and onion rings and gulping beers, ladies sitting at tables with salads and soups. He drew up next to Sunny as she placed a tray of sandwiches on the bar. Her eyes met his and her heart went into overdrive. Elvis sang about loving tender and sweet and she wanted to kiss him—Gray, not Elvis—so badly she felt dizzy.

Gray smiled. All day she'd wanted that smile. He nodded at the roomful of customers. "More than one woman didn't cook dinner tonight. Babysitters and Durango delivery pizza must be doing a land-office business."

One young cowboy said, "Hey, Gray. Find your brother yet?"

Gray stuffed his hands into his jeans pockets and leaned against the bar. Rugged, gorgeous and irresistible. But she had to resist. He said, "Got Dillon this afternoon. He blistered the phone lines with some creative swearing and is headed back ASAP, probably with a fistful of speeding tickets."

"'Bout time." Every cowboy at the bar nodded in agreement.

Gray picked a potato chip from the basket on the bar and said to Sunny, "Where's Elizabeth?"

"Upstairs. She's feeling yucky with the pregnancy, and Doc and Ms. Rose took the twins for the day. Next time I'll let Doc pick them up in his car like he suggested, instead of walking them to his place."

Maxine chuckled around a mouthful of chicken salad.

"Saw you out with the boys and Six. Every puddle in town between The Smokehouse and the clinic has four little shoe prints and four paw prints smack in the middle."

Gray's gaze washed over her. He rested his hand on the bar, nearly touching hers. She could feel the heat of his body on hers, his scent filling her head. His eyes turned chocolate brown and he swallowed hard, seeming to want her as much as she wanted him. "You're really busy tonight. Didn't think it would be this crowded with all the rain."

Norm handed Gray a beer and said, "Weather has nothing to do with it. Dillon McBride's twins and pretty, pregnant wife are staying upstairs. Nobody, man or woman, wants to miss tonight when he gets back to town. Going to be better fireworks here than yesterday's."

Sunny tore her gaze from Gray and focused on Norm. Looking at Gray and knowing she could never have him was torture. "What's Dillon like?"

Everyone laughed and Norm offered, "Gray with a rocket up his butt."

Elizabeth came around the corner and approached as if walking on a wet tile floor. Gingerly she sat at the bar away from most of the food. "Okay, bartender, pour me something mean and ornery." She eyed Gray. "It's going to be a rough night. The McBride brothers are in town."

Gray went over and kissed her on the cheek as Norm passed her a glass of sparkling water, a pack of soda crackers and a napkin.

Sunny snatched Elizabeth's hand. "Keeping anything in your stomach?"

"Do stale pretzels count? I felt this way with the boys. If they weren't kicking me and poking me and sitting right on my kidneys—wasn't it nice I have one for each—they were making me lose my lunch. If I bring another McBride man into the world I'm shipping him back where he came from."

Every woman nodded in sympathy and Sunny pointed to the door. "Think Dillon will show?"

Elizabeth fluffed the paper napkin onto her lap and sipped the water. "*Show* is such a calm word."

As if proving her right, the bar door banged open, rattling the windows, shaking dust from the beams and framing Dillon McBride in the entrance.

Chapter Ten

Sunny and everyone else in The Smokehouse went still...except Elizabeth. She sipped water and munched crackers—the only sound in the saloon, since someone had pulled the plug on the jukebox. Who'd want to miss one word of soap opera Tranquility style?

Dillon scowled from the doorway. Was that steam curling from his Stetson? His piercing black gaze zeroed in on Elizabeth as if she wore a homing device. He stomped his way to his wife, boots thudding against the hardwood floor. "Elizabeth Randall-McBride, what the hell do you think you're doing?"

"Hello, Dillon. Have a nice business trip, dear?"

His face reddened to the same color as Gray's when Sunny tied him to the post yesterday. Genetic characteristic or testosterone surge? Hard to tell.

Elizabeth held up her glass. "Join me?"

Dillon's eyes went bloodshot and Sunny remembered Gray's doing the very same thing.

"You're coming home with me this minute."

"Why would it matter? You're not around enough to know if I'm home or not, dear."

"Don't *dear* me, and you're my wife and you belong at home, dammit."

Genetic characteristic *and* testosterone surge. Sunny said, "No cussing at a pregnant lady in this bar."

"I'm not cussing at her—I'm cussing *because* of her, and I'll cuss when and where I please."

Sunny smiled sweetly. "I don't think so."

"Pack your bags, Liz. I'll get the boys."

"Do you remember what they look like, dear? You might pack the wrong ones."

His eyes narrowed. His teeth clenched. He growled, "I have a ranch to run, businesses to take care of. I can't be around as much as you think I should. I'll hire someone to help with the children."

Elizabeth put down her glass decisively and stood. She was much smaller than Dillon but no less mighty. She glared. She had a great glare. "I don't want hired help. I want you, at least some of the time, which means more than you're around now."

Sunny spread her arms wide and flashed a hopeful grin. "Why not let Gray help out?"

Gray shook his head with a not-now glint in his eyes and Dillon suddenly grinned. He walked over to Gray and slapped him on the back. "Well, hell. That's it. That's the exact answer we need. *Gray.* Why didn't I think of it before?"

Sunny suddenly felt the whole world go rosy. Birds sang, church bells chimed, she was giddy with happiness. No need for an election. She and Gray could be together and—

"Gray can baby-sit the boys."

Sunny sucked in a quick breath. *"What?"*

"He's great with them and they love him, and Lizzy can get some free time to herself."

Gray shrugged in an I-told-you-so fashion; Sunny felt all her hopes vanish into thin air and Elizabeth groused, "I'm not after free time, Dillon McBride. I'm looking for a husband beyond random physical acts of procreation. Gray is supposed to help you run the ranch. Don't you get it?"

Dillon's face pinched into hard lines. "I've run the Lazy K for years and don't see any reason to change now. Besides, I'm not the one complaining. Gray can help *you*. Everything's worked out. We're done here. Let's go."

Elizabeth fisted her hands on her hips. Every eye in the place focused on her. "I'm staying at The Smokehouse with Sunny and I'm not complaining. I'm trying to make the point that things have to change."

"I won't have my children raised over some burnedout sleazy bar."

"Hey," Sunny said, "watch what you're calling sleazy, buster."

"Liz, you're coming home, if I have to toss you over my shoulder and take you home."

Gray said, "That's not a real good idea, big brother."

Sunny drew up beside Elizabeth "No one's going to toss anyone anywhere. This is my bar and—"

"Your bar?" came a voice from the doorway.

Sunny froze. *That voice*…it sounded…familiar? Slowly she turned toward it…along with everyone else. A green-eyed, blond-haired woman in poison-green capris and white stretch halter top stood framed in the entrance. She grinned and gave Sunny a little finger wave. "Sophie? Is that really you? Ohmygod. Ohmygod!"

She ran over and hugged Sunny. "I couldn't imagine what in the world happened when you didn't come back to Reno. I tried calling the sheriff's office here and no one had seen you or even heard of you. It was like you vanished off the face of the earth. I kept making excuses for you at your office, and since this was where you were supposed to be, I thought I'd start looking here. But I had to be careful and drive the back roads at night in case Cement Sam and his merry men of concrete workers were on my tail." She gave a big grin. "And now you're here. This is fantastic. Ohmygod!"

Sunny felt a thick cloud lift from her brain. She recognized this woman…sort of. "I didn't vanish. My memory just did. *Who are you?*"

"Why haven't you sold the bar? Sam hasn't found me yet, but he's got to be close. And what in the world are you doing dressed in denim shorts and a tank top? I didn't think you owned denim. Where's your gray slacks, black top, loafers? You always wear loafers. Never leave home without them, and now you have on sandals. What's going on with you?" She frowned. "Why didn't you call me?"

Gray looked from the woman in the halter top to Sunny. Every eye in the saloon did the same, taking the heat off Elizabeth and Dillon for the moment. Gray asked, "Who in the hell's Sophie?"

The woman tsked and pointed her red manicured finger at Sunny. "What do you mean, *who's* Sophie? *She's* Sophie. Sophie Addison. Workaholic attorney and my best and dearest friend since we took on that bully Jeremy Frazer in kindergarten because he was beating up everyone. She came here to sell this saloon to pay off Cement Sam because I made a bet and took out a loan and didn't repay it and…" She wrinkled her nose and shook her head. "Well, that's another story and doesn't matter right now. All that really matters is that I found her, and Cement Sam hasn't found us." She beamed.

Sunny…real Sunny…surveyed the room. "This place is sure better than the pictures that the attorney sent to me." She tapped her finger to her pink-frosted lips. "You know, maybe we can get more money for it than I thought. I saw an article in *Reader's Digest* on how not to get swindled in selling property. Don't you just love that *Reader's Digest?*"

Sophie caught a glimpse of herself in the mirror behind the bar. "I'm Sophie Addison?" She pulled herself onto a bar stool so she wouldn't collapse onto the floor.

"Well, who'd you think you were?"

She looked back to Sunny, the real Sunny. "You."

"Me?" Sunny's green eyes sparkled and she

laughed, the sound filling the saloon. Tears trailed down her cheeks. "You really thought you were a Reno showgirl? Oh, I wish I'd been around to see that. Sophie Addison finally cuts loose and I miss it. After all these years of my trying to get you to have some fun, you do and I'm not here to take pictures."

Her face took on a coy expression and she shook her finger and shot Sophie a wide-eyed look. "You did have fun, didn't you?"

She thought of Gray and Elizabeth and the twins and Doc and her cowboys and the rodeo. A smile fell across her lips. "Yeah, I had fun. Probably the best time of my life, though it's still hard to remember my other life."

"Don't try too hard. It's not worth it—believe me. And I bet I can guess why you had a good time here." Real Sunny sauntered over to Gray and held out her hand. "And *who* are you, handsome?"

Gray took the offered hand. "Gray McBride." He nodded. "This is Dillon, my brother, and Elizabeth, my sister-in-law, and all these fine folks live here, as well. Welcome to Tranquility."

She held Gray's hand longer than necessary and batted her eyelashes. Sophie's insides tightened as bits and pieces of being a lawyer and her apartment and Auntie—her real auntie—came flooding back. She was just a boring attorney.

Sunny was exactly the kind of girl Gray liked. The kind of women he'd always been attracted to. The kind of woman Sophie thought she was but wasn't and never would be no matter how many attacks of amnesia she acquired.

Sunny grinned at Gray. "Mighty glad to be here. Especially since I can sell the saloon, make peace with Sam and get on with my life."

Sophie shook her head, trying to take everything in and suddenly realizing where all this was headed. "You...you really intend to sell The Smokehouse?"

"Well, it's not like I have a choice. It's either sell or wind up in some expressway or wall in some ballpark. That's why you came. You must have gotten amnesia real bad. Anyway, now that you know who you are and who I am and Sam hasn't used the cement part of his elegant title, there's still time to make things right. Right?"

Dillon came to Elizabeth. "See? The Smokehouse is sold, you have no place to stay and you can come home now. Let's get out of here."

Elizabeth poked Dillon in the chest with her index finger. "It's not sold yet."

"Ah, hell!" Dillon stomped back across the saloon to the door and slammed it behind him.

Elizabeth grinned smugly, reclaimed her place at the bar and took a triumphant swig of sparkling water. The women cheered, the men groused and swilled beer and Gray came to Sophie and draped his arm around her shoulders. It felt good, wonderful, in fact. Supportive. She needed support right now because she just might fall flat on her face. He said, "I think we all deserve another round of drinks."

This time everyone cheered and started talking and gabbing. Sunny pinched a strand of Sophie's hair. "You cut it. A lot." She peered at Sophie, concern in her eyes. "Are you okay?" She smiled up at Gray and gave a sexy wink, one Sophie couldn't master no matter who she thought she was. Some things were simply inborn. Sunny continued, "But it seems you've been in very, very good hands while you were here, so I'm guessing you're fine and dandy."

Sophie stood. Patrons watched her and Gray. "We— Gray and I—are merely friends. He's running for mayor. We…we planned a rodeo together, for the town on the Fourth of July. It was a big success."

"*You* planned a rodeo?" Sunny said, a skeptical edge in her voice. "With cows and horses and things that smell?"

"It fit the demographics and there was a reason. Well, there were several. And that's how Gray and I got to be *friends*. Just friends." She sucker punched his arm and grinned like one of the guys.

Gray looked at her as if she'd lost her mind—even more than she already had—and Sunny said, "Right." She let out a chuckle. "You never could lie worth spit, you know."

Sunny sat down at a table and pulled Sophie with her. Gray turned his attention to a long neck Art slipped into his hand. Sunny said, "You really haven't seen Sam here? I think he broke into my apartment, tore the place apart and took the information I had about this saloon. I'm surprised he didn't follow you here when he couldn't find me in Reno. I didn't know what that man was up to. That's why I had to be careful getting here."

"I've run into his henchmen a few times. They thought I was you. Our appearances are enough alike and everyone else around here thought I was Sunny Kelly. 'Course, if Sam himself had shown up he would have known the difference."

Sunny fluffed her golden curls. "I bet he shows up now. That money's way overdue. The only reason he's held off is that he wants the saloon sold so he can get the ten grand. A corpse can't pay up."

Sophie sat back in her chair. "We'll settle up with Sam when he shows and then head on back to Reno."

Sunny hitched her chin at Gray. "If that's what you really want to do. I lost my job at the Silver Bullet since I was gone so long."

Sophie grabbed her friend's hand and held it. "Holy cow. My job? Did anyone from Burns, Lock, Trenton and Fowler call looking for me?"

"Oh, yeah. I told them there was a death in the family. Figured that wasn't much of a lie with Sam on the loose, my bacon on the line and you and me being almost sisters."

Sophie added some sternness to her voice. "If you ever, *ever*, bet on another horse or borrow money from—"

"My borrowing days are over." Sunny held up her hands in surrender. "I'm turning over a new leaf." She grinned and nodded at Gray as he talked to Art. "Seems to me you turned over a new leaf, too. You're dressing different, having fun, and you've got yourself one dynamite cowboy. Way to go, girl. I always knew you could do it."

Sophie heaved a sigh. "I didn't do anything. Gray doesn't know me...at least not the real me. He knows an interesting, fireball saloon keeper. Not a stuffed-shirt attorney."

She could almost feel Gray slipping away from her, getting more distant by the minute. "I'm not his type at all. Not really."

Sunny patted her hand. "Gray McBride has the hots for you, honey. I can see it in his eyes. A mix-up of names doesn't matter squat to a man like him. He's the kind who knows what he wants and goes after it like a duck after a june bug." She grinned. "You're the june bug."

Sophie spread her hands, palms up. "I thought I was a showgirl, so I acted the part. But it was *all* just an act. The shorts, the idea of me knowing about saloons. Not the real me. He's got the wrong bug."

"That's what you think. Before, you never cared about anything but being a success and making your auntie proud. And she is, I'm sure of that. But it's time to find the real Sophie Addison. Auntie would have wanted that more than anything for you."

Sunny stood. "Now, point me toward the nearest bed-and-breakfast. I'm bushed. I don't need to hide out anymore. If Sam does find me, I'll tell him we're selling this saloon tomorrow to the town for their fire department and he can have his check."

Sophie nodded, feeling more of her dreams sliding away. In some ways it was as if the past two and a half weeks had never existed. Then she eyed Gray—dilapidated Stetson, broad shoulders, fine-fitting jeans, fabulous uncle, family man, her hero on more than one occasion. That time had happened, all right. *And along the way she'd fallen in love with Gray McBride.*

Terrific. In the past ten minutes thing had gone from bad to worse to even worse than that. Before, she couldn't have Gray because of the blasted election and she was a saloon keeper and showgirl, not some respectable woman who would enhance his chances. Well, now she was that respectable woman, but not the wild, fun-filled type of gal Gray McBride fell for at all. "I'll take you over to Bulah's House of Slumber."

Sunny lifted an eyebrow. "Huh?"

"It's a bed-and-breakfast. Bulah's just a colorful character. The rooms are decorated like Texas brothels of old, and wait till you taste Bulah's blueberry muffins. To die for…or at least gain a pound or two for."

They got up and headed arm-in-arm for the doorway. Sunny asked, "How'd this place get fixed up? The note from the bank attorney said it was in disrepair. Doesn't look in disrepair to me."

"It…" Sophie thought of all the work and worry she and the cowboys had put into saving The Smokehouse. "It just sort of happened." She smiled at Sunny. "Tomorrow we sell, Sam gets his money, Gray McBride will get elected mayor and everyone lives happily ever after."

Sunny pushed open the front door of the saloon and walked down the steps. "What's this saloon have to do with Gray getting elected mayor?"

Sophie laughed. "I'll tell you about it over a bag of Oreos and a Coke." Everything was back to normal, just as it had been before she'd landed in Tranquility, Texas, and met Gray McBride.

Trouble was…she'd met Gray McBride.

SOPHIE SAT on the bar stool and gazed at herself in the mirror behind the bar. At 3:00 a.m., with all the lights out, she couldn't get a clear reflection, just kind of a hazy one. That fit, since she felt hazy about everything that had gone on tonight. *Who the heck was she?*

Oh, she knew her real name, but that was it. Sophie Addison wasn't the same person now as the one who'd caught the red-eye in Reno, flown to Dallas and rented a car with bad AC. She laughed, remembering the pink spandex outfit she'd bought to keep cool. No wonder Gray thought she was Sunny.

"Sophie?" said Gray from the doorway. She turned on the stool and her gaze met his even through the darkness. She could feel his presence as much as see his silhouette. Big, strong, sexy as hell, great guy and friend. Yeah, she loved him, all right.

"What are you doing, sitting here by yourself?"

"Thinking about…stuff. Why are you here?"

"Sunny hasn't paid off this Sam guy yet, and until she does there's no telling what he'll try." Gray closed the door quietly behind him. "Do you remember every-thing now?"

She shrugged as he sat down on the stool beside her. Just having him near felt wonderful, and she'd better enjoy it now because tomorrow she, along with Sunny, was out of here, back to the real world. To lonely, bor-ing, corporate reports and forecasts she suddenly didn't care about at all. "There's not that much to remember. I'm a financial attorney. End of story."

"Guess that means you know more than the *Reader's Digest* version of law." He smiled and gave her a shoulder nudge.

"On occasion." She nudged him back and chuckled. "I had an aunt, like Sunny's. Except Auntie raised me along with every stray anything and anyone who came her way. She'd patch them up mentally and physically and send them on their way. Auntie saved a lot of peo-ple. Did a lot of good."

Gray set his hat to the back of his head. "Well, that explains things. Bessy was more of a 'bleed the saloon dry and bet the profits in Las Vegas' aunt." He pulled in a deep breath and took her hand. "You don't seem very happy about all this remembering."

"Tomorrow we sell The Smokehouse. Bad news for me, good for you. Now The Smokehouse can be part of the firehouse…just like you originally planned."

"What about Art and Norm and Smitty and Jean and Clyde?"

She felt her throat tighten. "They all depended on me…on The Smokehouse. I don't know what I'm going to do, but maybe I can find them jobs here or in Reno. We had plans for The Smokehouse. Big plans and now…"

He kissed her temple, making her insides warm with wanting him. *Too bad!*

"I'll help you make other plans for them…and for us. You and I can finally be together."

She stared at him through the dim light from the porch. "Us?"

He turned sideways on the stool and looked straight into her eyes. "Don't you see? Everything's changed and some of it's for the better. You're an attorney. From the sounds of it, a good one with a fine reputation. You're not a saloon keeper and a showgirl from Reno. Not that I mind those things, but the citizens need to believe I've moved on to someone like you. I can win the election with you at my side because the good citizens will think I've matured, changed my ways, made a good choice. That I'm levelheaded and responsible. They'll think I'm attracted to you now, as an attorney. They won't know it started when I thought you were Sunny Kelly, saloon keeper and showgirl."

"But that's the trouble. You did fall for me as Sunny Kelly, and she doesn't exist."

He shook his head. "You lost me."

She sighed, letting his words sink in. "Yeah."

"We're perfect together. I've never met anyone like you. I'm really alive when I'm around you, not just going through the motions. I'm crazy about you, Sophie. Have been for a long time but couldn't act on it. Now I can."

"You're crazy about the woman you thought I was. You don't know diddly about me. Not the real me. I'm not the person you've talked to and argued with and made love to. I'm a boring lawyer. A finance geek. I play with numbers and I'm not a flamboyant showgirl, someone you'd be interested in. If you met me when I was me you'd just walk on by." She shook her head and gave a sad laugh. "How confusing is that?"

Gray framed her face with his hands. "You got this all wrong. I'd never just walk past you."

She slid from the stool. "The Sunny Kelly you're attracted to vanished when the real Sunny Kelly walked through the door."

Gray stood, his eyes boring into hers. "Like hell. She's right here in front of me, flesh and bones." He gave her a little grin. "Very nice flesh and bones, I might add." He kissed her. "Nothing's changed except now we can be together. I win the election and prove to Dillon once and for all I can help run the ranch, and he'll hand over some of the responsibility. Elizabeth will be thrilled and so will the whole damn town. Guys will realize they have to give in a little and will stop sleeping on the couch. It may take a few months, but it'll happen. Everything's perfect."

This time she kissed him, committing to memory the feel of his warm lips on hers, the feel of his body only inches away. "It's a perfect fairy tale. After the saloon's sold tomorrow afternoon, Sunny and I are heading back to Reno. There's no reason for me to stay."

"What about me? Stay for me. Till after the election.

You're confused now, that's all. In a couple of days you'll see how right we are for each other. I'll make it right, I swear."

"You can't. And I can't stay." *Because it hurts too much to be with you and know I can't have you.* Not that she could tell him that, because then he'd try all the harder to make them work when it was impossible; she wasn't the woman he'd fallen for. "I've got a job to get back to in Reno."

She turned and headed for the steps to the apartment. It was over, done. *Everything* was over and done. Amnesia was bad, remembering worse.

He caught up with her and turned her around. His eyes dark, his voice firm and unyielding, determination etched across his face. "Someway, somehow, I'll get you to believe that we belong together, Sophie Addison."

Chapter Eleven

The next morning, Gray pulled his truck to a gravel-spitting stop in front of the bank. Was he too late? Had Sophie already sold The Smokehouse? He hoped not, because he had to convince her not to do it.

After thinking about it all night, he realized that as long as the saloon was around with Smitty, Norm, Art, Jean and Clyde, Sophie wouldn't leave. She'd taken them in and she wouldn't abandon them outright. She'd help them, hang around for a while, get them squared away on how to run the place. And that would give Gray time to convince her...

Convince her of what? Damn good question. He'd figure it out later. The only thing he was sure of now was he didn't want her to leave Tranquility.

He ran inside the bank and found the wood-paneled room that seemed two sizes too small for all the people it held. The Smokehouse meant a lot to these people. Norm, Art, Smitty and Clyde stood against the far wall. He glanced at Sunny, then Sophie, both as gloomy as rain at midnight. Somehow he had to set things right. "Don't sell the saloon. It's a bad idea. For everyone."

The bank manager put down his pen and gave Gray a blank look. Actually, it was the bleary-eyed look he always had, probably from counting all that money. Gray waved his hand across the room. "The bank will make more from The Smokehouse as an operating business than selling it outright. Sunny and Sophie, along with Art, Norm, Smitty, Jean and Clyde, can make a go of the place. They already have. Sophie has the business know-how and The Smokehouse could be an even bigger success and bring more revenue to the town."

Elizabeth looked at him as if he'd sprouted another head. She tapped her pencil on the table. "Dear brother-in-law, selling The Smokehouse to the town and making it part of the firehouse was your idea. *Remember?*"

"Yeah." He took off his hat and raked his hair, feeling antsy as a cat in a dog pound. Impromptu stints of blabbering weren't exactly his thing. What the hell was he doing in politics? That was filled with all kinds of blabbering. "The town needs The Smokehouse as a social meeting place. There are no other bars in town and we all know how much business is conducted here."

Sophie stood. She braced her arms on the table and leaned toward him. "Maybe my amnesia's contagious and you got it. You built your campaign around closing down The Smokehouse and selling it. We—you and me—fought over that very issue many times.

Blackmail, coercion and arm-twisting were involved. Any of this sound familiar? What happened to make you change your mind?"

Yeah, it sounded familiar, and what happened was that he realized how much he'd miss Sophie if she left. His gaze connected with hers and the prospect of not seeing her again tore at his insides. "The Smokehouse is already profitable, not like before when Bessy had it. We can build another firehouse where the Gas 'n' Go used to be. What happened to that idea?"

Elizabeth held up the contract. "Tranquility requires a bigger firehouse, and using The Smokehouse is still the most economical way to expand because the building's already there." She arched an eyebrow. "That's why you suggested it in the first place. It was a good idea then and still is. Both parties—Sunny Kelly and the town council—agree to the sale. There's no reason not to proceed."

"And it better proceed damn quick," said a gravelly voice from the doorway. "Sunny Kelly better come up with a sizable chunk of change today. She owes me money and I'm tired of waiting around for it."

Everyone focused on the short man standing in the doorway. Gray pinstripe suit, crescent of gray hair, gray beady eyes. His skin had a gray cast. He entered followed by three men in T-shirts and baseball caps adorned with cement trucks. His own personal baseball team? Yeah, right.

Mr. Pinstripe straightened his gray tie. "Took us a while to find Ms. Kelly, then it turned out it wasn't her at all and we didn't know where she was. But now we do, thanks to the sheriff. He's a book of information on everything going on around here and likes talking about it."

Pinstripe glared at Sunny. "And you're not giving us the slip again. I'm keeping my eye on you." His eyes turned a darker gray, almost black. "My patience has worn real thin. Either Ms. Kelly pays up today or she—"

"No one's threatening anyone," Gray said as he came between the man and Sunny. Norm came up beside him. Then Art and Smitty and Clyde. The baseball boys went elbow to elbow next to their boss. Showdown at the Tranquility Bank and Trust.

"All right. All right." Sunny stood and held out her hands as if trying to stop two trains ready to collide head-on. "Everybody just back off. This is my problem and I'm going to fix it. I have to sell the saloon. I owe Sam money, fair and square. I'm going to pay him off now."

She smiled at Gray, Norm, Art, Smitty and Clyde. "I appreciate you all standing up for me. No man's ever done that for me before." Her eyes misted and her voice had a faint tremor as she continued, "Mostly men just whistle and make off-color comments, but you guys… You cowboys are the best." She pulled in a breath and turned to Elizabeth. "Hand me the papers and let's get this over with."

"No, wait," Gray blurted. "I'll buy the saloon. I'll pay more than the town will."

"No, you won't." Sophie spread her arms wide. "Ralph Nester will eat you alive. He's just waiting for you to do something like this so he can pounce like the flying roach he is. You'll never win the election and be mayor and then what happens to Elizabeth and the twins and the new baby?"

· Gray gritted his teeth. If he bought the saloon, it would look as if he did it to assure his campaign promise of making The Smokehouse part of the firehouse and he was buying his way into office. He'd play straight into Nester's hands, who'd made a point of Gray's being wealthy while he, Nester, was one of the common good old boys. Ha! *Good for nothing was more like it.*

Gray clenched and unclenched his hands. Buying The Smokehouse would make him lose the election and he'd let his family down. If he didn't buy it, he'd lose Sophie today, right now, for sure. Compared with this, riding bulls was a snap. You stayed on or you fell off. End of story. No big decisions.

Sunny took the pen and signed the papers, handed them to Elizabeth, who gave her a check for a little over ten grand, and another check to the bank to pay off the mortgage and the loans. The whole transaction took less than two minutes and Gray felt his life turn upside down.

Mr. Cement and his baseball team left, followed by the bank manager, who seemed relieved the whole mess was over. Sophie turned to the cowboys against the wall. "I'm going to make some phone calls about getting you all jobs in Reno. I know you'd rather stay here, but...but my connections are in Reno. You'll love Reno. It's a great town."

"Wait," Gray said, not ready to see his plans fall apart. "We should all at least have one last drink at The Smokehouse. A toast."

Sophie shrugged. "I'm not in much of a toasting kind of mood." Before Gray could offer a rebuttal, she was out the door.

Gray nodded at the others. "Drinks on me."

Elizabeth grinned. "Since the town now owns the saloon, the drinks are on them."

The cowboys and Sunny and Elizabeth followed Gray in funeral-procession silence to The Smokehouse. Their footsteps on the porch sounded hollow and depressing. He plopped down hard on a stool at the bar and Norm passed out long necks and sparkling water to Jean and Elizabeth. Norm raised his beer. "To The Smokehouse, to dreams and to friendships. The stuff life's made of."

They gulped, and Norm said, "*Now*, what are we all going to do?"

Elizabeth peered at Gray. "Well, *somebody* better wake up and do something. This nonsense has gone on long enough."

His gaze met Elizabeth's. What the hell did she mean by that?

Smitty put his arm around Jean. "I suppose we're going to Reno. We got a baby on the way, and there's not much work here for a washed-up cowboy like me."

Gray paced. "I can use you guys at the Lazy K. There's always work that needs—"

"Not for us," Smitty cut in, bringing Gray's pacing to a halt. He thumped Gray on the back. "That's why we never came to you for jobs. I've got a bum arm." He nodded at the other guys. "They aren't much better. We can't do cowboy kind of work any longer, Gray. It wouldn't be right for you and the rest of your hands, and we wouldn't feel right about it, either."

Art shook his head. "Odd jobs are tough to come by. We can get some training, but that takes time, and what do we do for money till then?"

Norm and Clyde nodded in agreement and Gray gulped his beer. "This isn't right. I've known you all for a long time." He turned to Smitty and Jean. "And I can't believe you two really don't want to raise your baby here, in Tranquility. You were married here, have friends here. And then there's Sophie."

He took another drink, then paced, feeling completely rotten. Beer had never tasted this bad. *Blah.* What the heck was wrong with him? He loved beer. Considered it the fourth food group. "She can't go back to being an attorney. She'll shrivel up and die as an attorney. None of us wants to see her go. She's a part of this town. Kind and caring and taking on everyone's problems, making them her own. There wouldn't be a Smokehouse without her, or a rodeo or a wedding reception. There wouldn't have been near the fun and excitement around here."

He paced the other way. "And what is she going to

do with Six? She can't take him back to an apartment. No apartment complex is going to let Six in. What would he do there? And what about the twins? They'll miss her, and—"

He stopped and looked back at the others, who were staring at him, grinning like jack-o'-lanterns on Halloween night. Smitty chuckled. "Well, dang. The mighty has finally fallen. You're in love with Sophie Addison."

Gray felt his jaw drop to the floor, or so it seemed. "That's crazy. Insane. I like Sophie. Everybody does. That doesn't mean I'm in love with her. You know me…" He flashed a macho grin, the kind that had sent more than one gal into a tizzy. He gave a cocky swagger. He needed to prove a point to the others…and himself. Smitty had it all wrong. "I'm the guy with the little black book, the guy who plays the field. I enjoy women—all women, and all their wonderful attributes—wherever I go. Always have. Sophie Addison's just another gal who happened along. Sure she's pretty. And she's smart and exciting and—"

"Why did you not want me to sell the bar?" Sunny asked. Then answered her own question with, "Because you knew it would keep Sophie here."

"And," Elizabeth added, "you want her here because you love her. Why else would you throw your campaign promises about expanding the firehouse to the wind? You were willing to do anything to get her to stay."

Gray felt as if he'd been hit upside the head with a

brick. "Oh, damn." He sat down, waiting for the room to stop spinning. He forgot to breathe. He eyed one of his friends, then the other. "Sophie?" He swallowed. "She's...she's leaving. What am I going to do? That can't happen."

Elizabeth laughed. "You stop her, of course."

"How? The Smokehouse is gone—the one thing, aside from the cowboys, that she'd stay around for. And I can't just tell her how...how I feel. She'll never believe me. Hell, she doesn't think I'd even notice her. That I'd walk right by her. Can you imagine any man walking right by Sophie without noticing? Though I better not catch any man noticing too much while I'm around."

This time Clyde laughed. "Oh, boy. You've got it bad."

Gray huffed and looked at each one of them. "That's all you can say—*I've got it bad*? A little advice would be good here. A few suggestions would be nice. Heaven knows all of you are ready to give your opinions on every other thing around here. I don't have a clue what to do to make Sophie stay."

Sunny, Smitty, Jean, Art, Norm, Elizabeth and Clyde clinked their bottles together and Smitty said, "To love and all the problems getting there. Good luck, Gray McBride. We can give you that because you sure as hell are going to need it." He grinned at Jean. "Just like the rest of us."

Chapter Twelve

Gray stomped up the steps of his house. Things had to change—he had to change—or he'd never get Sophie Addison to believe he loved her. "Dillon? Where the devil are you?"

"Kitchen. Stop yelling like a wounded buffalo. You'll wake the dead."

Gray came around the corner as Dillon took a bite of a sandwich. He glanced up, chewed and swallowed a gulp of milk. His eyes filled with concern. "Are the kids and Lizzy okay?"

"Yeah, they're fine."

Dillon grinned. "Good. Gave me a start there, little brother." He started to get up, but Gray put a firm hand on his shoulder, keeping him in place. "You better sit down for this." Gray pulled in a deep breath. "Starting Monday, I'm doing the cattle auctions that are farther away then fifty miles. I think our net operating loss needs to be readjusted by selling off some assets and I'm meeting with the accountants every two weeks to go over expenditures. We're overextended in oil production and should consider alternative sources of energy for investment. I just bought the Powder Keg for one hell of a lot of money, so when the check comes through, don't rupture a spleen over the number of zeros. Consider it as diversification, or not. I don't care what you consider it as. I intend to marry Sophie Addison, and if you've got a problem with any of this, tough, because that's the way it's going to be."

Dillon put a pickle on his sandwich, bit and said around a mouthful, "'Bout damn time."

"That's it? That's all you've got to say? What the hell's that supposed to mean?"

Dillon wiped his mouth with the back of his hand and stood. "I'm surprised you know as much about our holdings as you do."

"You've put me on copy for quarterly reports as long as I can remember. You just assumed I couldn't read. And it's about damn time for what?"

Dillon carried his dish to the sink. "Ranching and oil are a rough business. Getting worse all the time. If you don't take what's coming to you, someone else will get it before you know what's happened and you're screwed."

Dillon leveled Gray a hard look. "You have a business degree, but if you couldn't stand up to me, how would you ever stand up to anyone else in negotiating business dealings? It requires more than a degree to get the job done in the real world these days."

Dillon leaned against the counter. "Family loyalty is a fine thing. But it isn't worth squat if you can't get your own life squared away. When you go back into town, tell Lizzy everything worked the way we planned and I'm coming for her and the boys. Tell her to buy some new frillies over at Silk and Lace. I'm in the mood." He grinned and laughed. "And I'm betting she is, too. Been away too damn long."

"Let me get this straight. You *wanted* me to stand up to you, and Elizabeth was *in* on this?"

Dillon rinsed out the glass and put it in the dishwasher. "We got kind of desperate for you to do something with the new baby on the way. Thought us splitting up would get you to come around if anything would. We hoped you'd feel a little pressure about taking on some responsibility around here to push Lizzy and me back together." He shrugged as he added the plate to the dishwasher. "Though the whole town hopping on the bandwagon was a bit of a surprise."

He chuckled as he measured out detergent. "I think what really got to you was deciding what you wanted most. Ms. Sophie Addison and winning the election. Women have that effect on men…at least, McBride men. I remember when Lizzy walked into my life and I didn't know which way was—"

Before Gray could stop himself, he turned Dillon around and punched him square in the jaw. His brother stumbled backward into the stove, knocking the coffeepot to the floor and spewing coffee across the white tile.

Dillon rubbed his chin as he steadied himself. "You still pack a punch, little brother." He rubbed again. "I better drop the 'little' part." He came to Gray, sidestepping the coffee, and touched the rim of his hat. "It's time you got a new hat, one of your own. You've lived under someone else's shadow long enough."

Dillon took their father's Stetson and placed it on top of the cabinet. He put his hand on Gray's shoulder. "You're a good brother. A good son. A fine man. Dad would be proud of you—I am. Being the oldest was hard at times. Being the youngest was worse. I knew what I had to do and just went ahead and did it. You had to make choices and hoped they worked out. You did good."

Gray realized that all his life he'd wanted Dillon to say that. No words had ever meant as much. His throat tightened; his heart swelled. Dillon gave him a bear hug, as if welcoming him from a long journey. And in some ways he was right.

He let go and folded his arms. "So when's the wedding?"

"Wedding?" Gray felt a slow grin fall across his mouth, making him happier than he'd ever been. He massaged the back of his neck. "Hell, I haven't even thought about a wedding. Right now I'm just trying to get Sophie to stay around. I don't think she knows who she really is." Gray grinned. "Any more than I did."

"Then I guess you'll have to help her out. And let her understand you want to be a part of it."

"Yeah, maybe I'll do just that."

Gray tipped his head and made for the door as Dillon called, "Good luck. And don't forget to tell Lizzy about the frillies."

SOPHIE SPREAD the papers out on top of the bar and turned to the cowboys. "Okay, here's what I found. Norm, I got you a bartending job at a nice Reno restaurant. Good tips, good section of town. Classy clientele. 'Course, you'll have to wear a tux."

"A tux?" His eyes doubled in size. "Me? I'm a cowboy, Sophie."

"Well, now you're a cowboy in a tux. It's a good job." She turned to Norm. "There's an opening at the Vegetarian Cuisine. A wonderful vegetarian restaurant in Reno. You'll be a sous-chef. You'll love it."

"A who what?"

"Sous-chef. Helper to the main chef."

He pointed to the back room. "No way. I had my own kitchen…unless Art horned in. I'm not taking orders from some sous guy. And what the hell's this cuisine stuff? And vegetarian? That means no meat. How can I make Dagwoods with no meat?"

Norm made a face that looked as if he'd swallowed a lemon, and Gray said from the doorway, "'Cuisine' is a fancy name for grub and a Dagwood with no meat is downright sinful. No roast beef, turkey, ham? What kind of sandwich is that?"

Sophie huffed, "It's a sandwich that will put a paycheck in his hand."

Gray leaned against the bar. "Why go to Reno when you can make the sandwiches you want here?"

Sophie massaged her temples, a headache threatening. "You're not making this easy, Gray. There is no *here*. The Smokehouse is history. Where else in town can Smitty and Norm and—"

He held up a piece of paper and Sunny snapped it from Gray's fingers. "Well, if this don't beat all. It's a bill of sale for The Smokehouse." She looked at Gray. "You went and bought The Smokehouse?" She grinned. "I'm starting to talk Texan already." She laughed and handed Gray back the paper. "How about giving me a job?" She winked at Clyde and he blushed. "I'm thinking about staying around Tranquility. I kind of like the company."

Sophie slid onto a stool and smacked the palm of her hand against her forehead. She closed her eyes and let out a deep sigh as Gray asked, "What are you doing?"

"Trying to get the amnesia to come back. Life was much easier then." She peeked open one eye. "You should try it. Maybe it will knock some sense into you. Now you'll never get elected mayor."

He sat down beside her. "I don't care."

She gave him a stern look. "You have to care. This is your town and Nester is going to ruin it and it's all because—" She scrunched up her nose in confusion. "Why did you buy The Smokehouse?"

"Nester's not going to ruin anything because Ms. Rose is going to get elected mayor."

She put her hand to his forehead. No fever that had cooked his brain. "Gray, Ms. Rose isn't even running."

"She'll be a write-in. I'm taking out an ad in the *Tranquility Times* endorsing her and listing all her qualifications…which are more and better than mine and

Nester's combined. This gives the women in Tranquility the voice and leadership they've been looking for. The men will vote for her, because if she loses, they know they'll be sleeping on the couch for the rest of their lives."

He turned to the cowboys and Sunny and Jean. "I've got a box of campaign posters for Ms. Rose in my truck. Got them run off this afternoon. Would you all mind putting them up around town? And when you come back, we better get this place ready for tonight. I've got a feeling business will be better than ever."

Sunny snatched Gray's chin between her thumb and forefinger and turned his face to hers. "You're going to run The Smokehouse?"

He went behind the bar and pulled a long neck from the fridge. "The most I'm going to run is in here from time to time to steal a brew." He pointed the bottle toward the four cowboys. "They're going to run it. We'll work out some profit-sharing strategies."

Smitty turned to Sophie. "What about you?"

Gray shook his head. "She's out of the picture."

"Moving back to Reno?"

Gray shook his head again. "Moving upstairs."

Sophie stood and faced him. "In your dreams. Whatever you decide to do here is your business, but home is in Reno."

"You just *think* your home's in Reno."

Smitty looked from Gray to Sophie and chimed in with, "I think this is a great time for the rest of us to hang up those posters and let you two settle this. You don't need us around to chaperone."

He and Jean, Norm, Art, Clyde and Sunny paraded out the door as Sophie said to Gray, "Buying the saloon is a really bad financial decision. Dillon's got to be having a conniption you did it. And what'll happen to the firehouse now? Maybe we should all get out our garden hoses and ladders and forget the whole blasted thing. It's too much of a hassle."

"Dillon and I have an…understanding. Elizabeth and the twins are moving back home. The town council found unexpected funds and is building the new firehouse where Lucky Tanner's Gas 'n' Go was." He shrugged. "Someone blew it up. There's a vacant lot there now. Imagine that."

"God works in mysterious ways." She tilted her head. "Is that why you bought the saloon—to give the town more money to build the firehouse?"

"I bought the saloon for you."

"Me? I'm a lawyer, not a barkeep. I'm not suited to run a saloon, at least not for the long run. A couple of week were fun, but—"

"Actually, you haven't been doing it in the short run, either."

She put her hands on her hips. "Looks like a saloon, smells like a saloon. Bottles, stools, a bar. Gray, trust me, it's a saloon, and I ran it."

"You're the one who hired people…people who needed jobs…to run it for you. That's what you do and who you are. You help people and make them productive by setting up a plan, whether it's a business plan or wedding plan or rodeo plan. When everyone else asks why, you think why not and make it happen, and along the way you make people feel successful and good about themselves." He kissed her forehead. "You're Auntie."

She spread her hands wide. "I'm a lawyer."

"So you're Auntie with a law degree. You're all the more effective at what you do. Open an office upstairs and do what you do best…get people through hard patches so they can make successes of their lives. You heard the women here the other night. Beauty parlors, going back to school, and that's just the beginning. They have big dreams and they'll need your input to have their ideas be a success. The town will pay you…especially with Ms. Rose in charge. You won't get rich, but you'll make a difference. Isn't that what you really want to do with you life?"

She wasn't sure. Right now she wasn't sure of anything, least of all herself. "What's in this for you, besides owning a saloon?"

His eyes darkened and he smiled.

Her heart skipped a beat. She wanted to believe in him more than anything else in the world.

"I love you."

She let out a long sigh, her heart breaking because she knew he didn't love her…not really. How could he? "We've been through this, Gray. You don't know me. You can't love someone you don't know."

He gently took her face in his strong hands. He

brushed her lips with his. "I *do* know you. All the things I just told you about yourself prove it. I probably know you better than you know yourself right now because I've seen the real Sophie Addison doing all the things she wants to do, and I want to spend the rest of my life with her. If you're not ready to deal with that, fine. But if you stay in Tranquility maybe someday you will. We're good together, Sophie. The best."

He got down on one knee and looked up at her, happy and confident, and she felt that way, too. "Marry me. Maybe not now or next month, but whenever you're ready. I swear I'll make you the happiest woman on earth if it takes all my life."

She knelt beside him, folding his hands in hers. "You already have made me happy. I love you. I think I have since I woke up in Doc's clinic. In some ways the amnesia got me to see things clearer, do things I always wanted to do."

He grinned. "You always wanted to marry a cowboy?"

"I wanted to find the most wonderful man on earth and spend my life with him." She kissed him. "And I have."

Turn the page for a preview of next month's American Romance titles!

We hope these brief excerpts will whet your appetite for all four of January's books...

One Good Man by Charlotte Douglas (#1049) is the second title in this popular author's ongoing series, "A Place to Call Home." Charlotte Douglas creates a wonderful sense of home and community in these stories.

Jeff Davidson eased deeper into the shadows of the gift shop. Thanks to his Special Operations experience, the former Marine shifted his six-foot-two, one-hundred-eighty pounds with undetectable stealth. But his military training offered no tactics to deal with the domestic firefight raging a few feet away.

With a stillness usually reserved for covert insertions into enemy territory, he peered through a narrow slit between the handmade quilts, rustic birdhouses and woven willow baskets that covered the shop's display shelves.

On the other side of the merchandise in the seating area of the café, a slender teenager with a cascade of straight platinum hair yelled at her mother, her words exploding like a barrage from the muzzle of an M-16. "You are so not with it. Everyone I hang with has her navel pierced."

Jeff grimaced in silent disapproval. The kid should have her butt kicked, using that whiny, know-it-all tone toward her mom. Not that the girl's behavior was his business. He hadn't intended to eavesdrop. He'd come to Mountain Crafts and Café to talk business with Jodie Nathan, the owner, after her restaurant closed. Lingering until the staff left, he'd browsed the shelves of the gift section until she was alone.

But before he could make his presence known, fourteen-year-old Brittany had clattered down the stairs from their apartment over the store and confronted her mother.

"Your friends' navels are their mothers' concern, not mine." The struggle for calm was evident in Jodie's firm words, and the tired slump of her pretty shoulders suggested she'd waged this battle too many times. "You are my daughter, and as long as you live under my roof, you will follow my rules."

Was the kid blind? Jeff thought with disgust. Couldn't she see the tenderness and caring in her mother's remarkable hazel eyes? An ancient pain gnawed at his heart. He'd have given everything for such maternal love when he'd been a child, a teenager. Even now. Young Brittany Nathan had no idea how lucky she was.

Daddy by Choice by Marin Thomas (#1050). A "Fatherhood" story with a western slant. This exciting new author, who debuted with the delightful *The Cowboy and the Bride*, writes movingly and well about parent-child relationships…and, of course, romance!

JD wasn't sure if it was the bright sunlight bouncing off the petite blond head or the sparkling clean silver rental car that blinded him as he swung his black Ford truck into a parking space outside Lovie's café. Both the lady and the clean car stood out among the dusty, mud-splattered ranch vehicles lined up and down Main Street in Brandt's Corner.

Because of the oppressive West Texas heat wave blanketing the area, he shifted into Park and left the motor running. Without air-conditioning, the interior temperature would spike to a hundred degrees in sixty seconds flat, and he was in no hurry to get out.

He had some lookin' to do first.

A suit in the middle of July? He shook his head at the blonde's outfit. Pinstripe, no less. She wore her honey-colored hair in a fancy twist at the back of her neck, revealing a clean profile. Evidently, she got her haughty air from the high cheekbones.

All of her, from her wardrobe to her attitude, represented a privileged life. Privileged meant money. Money meant trouble.

His gut twisted. Since yesterday's phone call from this woman, his insides had festered as if he'd swallowed a handful of rusty fence nails.

Fear.

Fear of the unknown…the worst kind. He'd rather sit on the back of a rank rodeo bull than go head to head with her. Too bad he didn't have the option.

Table for Five by Kaitlyn Rice (#1051) is an example of our "In the Family" promotion—stories about the joys (and difficulties) of life with extended families. Kaitlyn Rice is a talented writer whose characters will stay with you long after you've finished this book.

Kyle Harper glanced at his watch and uttered a mild curse. He'd worked well past a decent quitting time again—an old habit that was apparently hard to break. Shoving the third-quarter sales reports into his attaché case, he closed his eyes, claiming a few seconds of peace before switching gears. He pictured a perfect gin martini, a late version of the television news and a bundle of hickory wood, already lit and crackling in the fireplace.

Heaven.

Or home, as he'd once known it.

Life didn't slow down for hard-luck times, and it didn't cater to wealth or power. Kyle could afford only a moment to ponder used-to-be's. He popped open his eyes and grabbed his cell phone, the fumbling sounds at the other end warned him about what to expect. "Grab the guns!" Kyle's father yelled. "There's a gang of shoot-'em-up guys headed into town!"

The Forgotten Cowboy by Kara Lennox (#1052). An unusual take on a popular kind of plot. Thanks to the heroine's amnesia, she doesn't recognize the cowboy in her life—which makes for some interesting and lively complications!

Willow Marsden studied the strange woman in her hospital room. She was an attractive female in her twenties, her beauty marred by a black eye and a bandage wound around her head. The woman looked unfamiliar; she was a complete stranger. Unfortunately, the stranger was in Willow's mirror.

She lay the mirror down with a long sigh. Prosopagnosia—that was the clinical name for her condition. She'd suffered a head injury during a car accident, which had damaged a very specific portion of her brain—the part that enabled humans to distinguish one face from another. For Willow, every face she saw was strange and new to her—even those of her closest friends and relatives.

"You're telling me I could be like this forever?"

Dr. Patel, her neurologist, shrugged helplessly. "Every recovery is different. You could snap back to normal in a matter of days, weeks, months, or…yes, the damage could be permanent."

"What about my short-term memory?" She couldn't even remember what she'd had for breakfast that morning.

Again that shrug. Why was it so difficult to get a straight answer out of a doctor?

Willow knew she should feel grateful to be alive, to be walking and talking with no disfiguring scars. Her car accident during last week's tornado had been a serious one, and she easily could have died if not for the speed and skill of her rescuers. Right now, though, she didn't feel grateful at all. Her plans and dreams were in serious jeopardy.

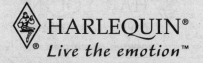

If you enjoyed what you just read,
then we've got an offer you can't resist!

Take 2 bestselling love stories FREE!
Plus get a FREE surprise gift!

Clip this page and mail it to Harlequin Reader Service®

IN U.S.A.	IN CANADA
3010 Walden Ave.	P.O. Box 609
P.O. Box 1867	Fort Erie, Ontario
Buffalo, N.Y. 14240-1867	L2A 5X3

YES! Please send me 2 free Harlequin American Romance® novels and my free surprise gift. After receiving them, if I don't wish to receive anymore, I can return the shipping statement marked cancel. If I don't cancel, I will receive 4 brand-new novels every month, before they're available in stores! In the U.S.A., bill me at the bargain price of $4.24 plus 25¢ shipping & handling per book and applicable sales tax, if any*. In Canada, bill me at the bargain price of $4.99 plus 25¢ shipping & handling per book and applicable taxes**. That's the complete price and a savings of at least 10% off the cover prices—what a great deal! I understand that accepting the 2 free books and gift places me under no obligation ever to buy any books. I can always return a shipment and cancel at any time. Even if I never buy another book from Harlequin, the 2 free books and gift are mine to keep forever.

154 HDN DZ7S
354 HDN DZ7T

Name	(PLEASE PRINT)
Address	Apt.#
City	State/Prov.	Zip/Postal Code

Not valid to current Harlequin American Romance® subscribers.

Want to try two free books from another series?
Call 1-800-873-8635 or visit www.morefreebooks.com.

* Terms and prices subject to change without notice. Sales tax applicable in N.Y.
** Canadian residents will be charged applicable provincial taxes and GST.
  All orders subject to approval. Offer limited to one per household.
  ® are registered trademarks owned and used by the trademark owner and or its licensee.

AMER04R   ©2004 Harlequin Enterprises Limited

Mother and Child Reunion

A *ministeries* from
2003 RITA® finalist

Jean Brashear

Coming Home

Cleo Channing's dreams were simple: the stable home and big, loving family she never had as a child. Malcolm Channing walked into her life and swept her off her feet and before long, she thought she had it all—three beautiful children in a charming house she would fill to the rafters with love.

Their firstborn was a troubled girl, though, and the strain on their family grew until finally, there was nothing left to do but for them to all go their separate ways.

Now their daughter has returned, and as the days pass, awareness grows in Cleo and Malcolm that their love never truly died.

Except, the treacherous issues that drove them apart in the first place remain....

Heartwarming stories with a sense of humor, genuine charm and emotion and lots of family!

On sale starting January 2005
Available wherever Harlequin books are sold.

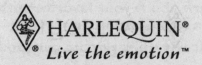

HARLEQUIN *Super*ROMANCE®

If you're looking for a fabulous read, reach for a Kathleen O'Brien book. You can't go wrong.
—Catherine Anderson,
New York Times *bestselling author*

THE HEROES OF HEYDAY

It's worth holding out for a hero....

Three brothers with different mothers. Brought together by their father's last act. The town of Heyday, Virginia, will never be the same—neither will they.

Coming soon from Harlequin Superromance and RITA® finalist Kathleen O'Brien—a compelling new trilogy.

The Saint (Harlequin Superromance #1231, October 2004)
The Sinner (Harlequin Superromance #1249, January 2005)
The Stranger (Harlequin Superromance #1266, April 2005)

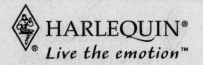

HARLEQUIN®
Live the emotion™

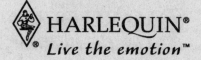